I walked into the kitchen. My mom was standing at the counter, singing to herself as she loaded watermelon chunks into the Cuisinart. I stared at her.

My mom glanced over at me. "Everything okay?"

I stood there, not saying a word.

"Skye? Are you okay? You look like you saw a ghost."

I turned and walked back into my room. As I closed my door, I wondered how it's possible that one person's entire world can change while the other person is still making watermelon soup.

tangled

CAROLYN MACKLER

An Imprint of HarperCollins*Publishers*

HarperTeen is an imprint of HarperCollins Publishers.

Tangled

Library of Congress Cataloging-in-Publication Data
Mackler, Carolyn.
    Tangled / Carolyn Mackler.— 1st ed.
        p.   cm.
    Summary: The lives of four very different teenagers become
entangled in ways that none of them could have imagined after a short
stay at a Caribbean resort.
    ISBN 978-0-06-173106-8
    [1. Interpersonal relations—Fiction.   2. Emotional problems—
Fiction.   3. Family   problems—Fiction.   4. Self-confidence—Fic-
tion.   5. Conduct of life—Fiction.   6. New York (State)—Fiction.]
PZ7.M2178   Tan2010   2009007286
[Fic]—dc22   CIP
                                                              AC

Typography by Ray Shappell

11   12   13   14   15   CG/BV   10 9 8 7 6 5 4 3 2 1
❖
First paperback edition, 2011

To Jodi Reamer, with so much gratitude

APRIL:

JENA'S STORY

one

Paradise sucked until I found the suicide note. And then it didn't suck at all. It was so good, in fact, that I thought maybe my entire life was finally going to change. And then, that last night, everything tanked. But somehow, over the next few months, my life did begin changing.

That's jumping way ahead, though.

I should start at the beginning, when my mom told me we were going to Paradise in the first place.

two

It was a typical Wednesday evening in Topeka, New York. Spring break was coming up next week, so I had nine minutes of homework, which I did while IMing my best friends, Ellie and Leora, surfing for celebrity gossip, and sending a virtual plate of snickerdoodles to my brother's ReaLife page. Then, since I *happened* to be on ReaLife, I checked out Samir Basu's online profile. And then, since I have no self-control, I opened every photo on his page and drooled waterfalls over his caramel cheekbones and milk-chocolate eyes. I lust after Samir and, yes, have even fantasized about how we'll gloriously merge cultures (me: Jewish; him: Indian) for our wedding ceremony. Never mind the trivial fact that when I pass Samir at school he rarely waves at me. Ellie, Leora, and I are still debating whether, during archery on Monday, Samir was coughing up a lugie or saying, "I love you forever, Jena Gornik." My best friends, those traitors, went for the mucus. One guess where I cast my vote.

Finally, I closed my future husband's ReaLife page, grabbed the Froot Loops, and parked in front of the TV. I wasn't watching a specific show, mostly just using it as background noise as I copied quotes into my everything book. I'm obsessed with quotes. You name the person—Albert Einstein (smart), Toni Morrison (very smart), Nicholas Sparks (pure genius)—and I've got one of their sayings. My everything book is a regular blank journal I bought last year. The cover is that famous black-and-white photo of the couple kissing outside Hôtel de Ville in Paris. I once googled the image and was crushed to learn that not only was the kiss *staged* using models, but the woman later sued the photographer for damages. I did my best to block those facts out.

Mostly I fill my everything book with quotes about love, life, heartbreak, and inspiration. In my sixteen years of life, I've had yet to experience love or heartbreak (or even much inspiration), so instead I stockpile other people's musings about those things. Sometimes I scribble strands of overheard conversations into my book. Now and then I tape in a note someone discarded in the halls of Topeka High School. You'd be surprised what you can find when you're a trash-picker. Two weeks ago, I scooped up a crumpled Post-it from the locker area outside the band room. *Do calc. Practice flute. Get bikini wax for Sat. p.m.* When I read that, I was like, *What?!!* I can guarantee that if I ever have to wax down yonder for some specific event, those other to-dos would fade into oblivion. But since I'm still in the math-and-music-practice stage, I must glean from other people's exciting lives, and it all goes into my everything book.

Around eleven thirty that Wednesday night, my mom got home. A few times a year, she has a big night out with her college roommate, Luce Wainscott. Luce lives in New York City, an hour and a quarter south of Topeka on the commuter train. Luce is insanely wealthy. When she takes my mom out, they go to an expensive restaurant and Luce orders a bottle of chardonnay and spends more on the appetizers than we probably do on an entire month of groceries. Luce even pays for my mom to take a car service back to Topeka. My mom always tries to split the tab, but Luce is so loaded (Texas oil fortune) it's a joke that my mom (a first-grade teacher) would plunk down her credit card.

"Is Dad sleeping?" my mom asked as she flopped onto the couch next to me.

"I think so," I said. My dad works at the junior high three towns away and has to wake up by five fifteen every morning. "I haven't heard from him in a while."

My mom kicked off her shoes and hoisted her feet onto the coffee table. "So he didn't tell you?"

"Tell me what?" I asked, vacuum-sucking a fleck of Froot Loops out of my braces.

"Where we're going for spring break," my mom said, smiling.

"Where *who's* going?"

My parents had next week off too. But with my brother, David, in college, we didn't have any extra money for vacations. The whopping plan so far was that I was going to take a bus to Binghamton and spend four days with Grandma Belle. That's my mom's mother. We bake kugel and watch the soaps and drive her Buick to every all-you-can-eat buffet in town. My mom is always saying we're a family of big-boned women, but Grandma Belle calls me luscious. I totally don't buy it, but she says someday I'll realize she's right.

"You and me, Jena," my mom said. "We're going to Paradise, a five-star resort in the Caribbean."

The Cari-*what*?

Before I could question the amount of chardonnay my mom had consumed, she went on to explain how, at dinner tonight, Luce mentioned that she'd reserved an enormous suite at Paradise next week and had tons of extra room and we should tag along. And so my mom whipped out her cell phone and called my dad, who bought the plane tickets and kept it secret from me all evening.

I was speechless. My mom never whips out her cell phone. My dad doesn't splurge on last-minute plane tickets. I wanted to ask my mom how come we're in a parallel universe where my life is exciting and my parents are cool. But something else was heavy on my mind.

"Is Skye coming?" I asked.

"Of course," my mom said. "That's the whole point."

"The whole point?"

"Luce and I will get time together and you and Skye can run around and have fun."

For one, I don't run. Not on a track. Not on a treadmill. And certainly not with Skye Wainscott. Luce's daughter is seventeen and beautiful and lives in Manhattan and has a gorgeous boyfriend and, to top it off, she has appeared in commercials and on TV shows. Ever since we were little, we've been stuck together when our moms hang out. But what the moms don't understand is that Skye basically ignores me. And so, naturally, I can't stop babbling around her. That's what I do when I'm uncomfortable. I feel a compulsive need to fill silent space.

My mom gave me the details of the trip. We'd fly to a small island in the Caribbean this Saturday and return the following Friday. All I could think to say was that my bathing suit from last summer doesn't fit anymore. My mom handed me her credit card and told me to check out the sales on Lands' End. Once she'd headed upstairs, I scooped up some cereal and thought about how Paradise could go two ways:

Paradise Won:

Skye and I would bond. She'd finally decide I was worthwhile and I, in turn, would cease my verbal diarrhea. Everything I said would sound suave and sophisticated. We'd go jogging on the beach and meet guys everywhere we went (but since Skye has a boyfriend they'd all be for me), and I'd get a butterscotch tan and my butt would miraculously become toned.

By the time I returned to Topeka High, the world would meet a whole new Jena Gornik. I'd no longer be pegged as a B-plus student in a school full of geniuses. The band director would bump me to first-chair clarinet. Samir Basu would shoot his arrow in my direction (metaphorically, of course) and we'd start going out and he'd ask me to the junior prom and I'd no longer be the only sixteen-year-old in Westchester County who's never been groped. Well, I did kiss a greasy, zit-specked guy at my cousin's bar mitzvah last year, but I'd really rather not count that one.

Or, more realistically:

Paradise Lost:

Skye would blow me off. My life would remain pathetic.

This is the real world, not a Nora Roberts novel, so I had a sneaking suspicion it'd be option number two. But sometimes, by the flickering glow of the TV screen, it's nice to dream a little.

three

The thing about walking through an airport with Skye Wainscott is that she's stunning. She's tall and willowy with a high forehead, a perfect nose, smooth skin, and long, curly black hair. She was wearing oversized sunglasses, cargo pants, and a delicate shirt that showed off her boobs (which are bigger than mine even though she's way skinnier. NOT fair.). The iPhone cord dangling out of her pocket topped off her casually perfect ensemble. And then, enter me. My chin had broken out the night before, so I was powdered like a funnel cake. I'd spent fifteen minutes blowing out my hair, and I'd obsessed about my clothes until I came up with an ensemble that seemed chic and urban in my bedroom mirror. But now, under the glaring lights of Kennedy airport, it all felt wrong.

It was a few minutes before seven. We'd just cleared security, and the moms were going in search of coffee. Skye wanted to get magazines for the flight and I was tagging along. I could tell that the guys we passed, plus a handful of women, were checking her out. Maybe they were trying to place her from one of her commercials or shows. I had to wonder what they made of me. Did they think I was Skye's friend? Unlikely. Did they think I was her sister? No. If we were related, we'd have at least a few genes in common. Did people think I was her maid? Do people even have maids anymore?

When we got to the newsstand, Skye grabbed *People* and *Entertainment Weekly* and began thumbing through *In Touch*. I stood next to her, browsing *In Touch* even though I get my celebrity dish from the blogs because it's cheaper and more immediate and, anyway, I was going to attempt to read *Dandelion Wine* on this plane ride. My brother gave it to me last month. Now that David is an American studies major, he's always trying to push books that have some greater meaning about our country. When he came home for Passover all he could blabber about was his "Cold War Culture" course and how if I really wanted to understand the contrasting viewpoints in

1950s America (did I ever say that?) I had to read *The Catcher in the Rye* alongside *Dandelion Wine*. I tore through *The Catcher in the Rye* (and developed a major crush on Holden Caulfield) but have only read the first page of *Dandelion Wine*. So far, so dull.

"Are you reading anything good?" I asked Skye.

"Mostly just scripts," she said without looking up.

"You mean movies? That's so cool."

Skye glanced at me, one eyebrow raised.

Shut up, Jena, I warned myself.

"I'm just saying," I said, "that it's amazing you get to *read* movies before they're actually made. I mean, who else gets to do that?"

Skye pushed a curl back from her face.

"Are you doing any interesting projects now?" I asked.

"Not really." Skye shrugged. "Just a lot of auditions."

"Anything I've heard of?" I pressed. Ellie, Leora, and I are obsessed with Skye's career. Every time Luce tells my mom that Skye is going to be on something, we watch it, even if it's just a thirty-second commercial. I'd never admit this to Skye, but she's our big connection to the glamorous world outside of Topeka.

"It's kind of early, you know?" Skye said.

"For what?"

"I'm not really in the mood to talk about work."

My cheeks burned in shame. I headed over to the cashier to buy gum, except a Twix bar began calling my name. I could imagine peeling off the caramel with my teeth, crunching hard on the cookie center. I slid the Twix and a pack of Trident across the counter and quickly gave the guy my money before Skye could see that not only do I act like a loser, but I eat like one too.

I ended up flying first class to Paradise.

When Skye and I met up with our moms at the gate, Luce insisted I trade tickets with her so she and my mom could sit together in coach. I looked at my mom like, *Is this okay?* but she shrugged and didn't say anything. My mom is weird around Luce. Sometimes it seems like she's being bossed around.

Skye and I boarded the plane early, with the other elite travelers. As we settled in our smooth leather seats and a flight attendant took our drink orders, I was having a majorly surreal moment. I couldn't believe I was headed to an island in the Caribbean. I figured I'd have to wait for my honeymoon (my honeymoon with Samir) for something like this. And not only that, but flying *first class*. For one, we never fly anywhere we could feasibly drive. For two, whenever we have flown, we go coach. As we're boarding the plane, my dad always wonders (way too loudly) who in their right mind would spend eight times the amount for extra ass room. It's totally embarrassing, especially since we're a family who could use the extra ass room.

"I can't believe this," I said as I buckled my seat belt.

Skye was in the window seat, her iPhone on the tray table. "Can't believe what?"

"First class. The Caribbean. I definitely didn't think this is how spring break was going to go. I was supposed to visit my grandma in Binghamton and spend my days obsessing about Samir Basu."

"Who's that?"

"A guy at school." I snorted. "My boyfriend in some alternate reality. Definitely not like how you have it with Matt."

Skye fiddled with her diamond-encrusted necklace. "I broke up with Matt."

"Oh my god! When? Why?"

"In March," Skye said.

Skye scrolled through her music. She didn't look

the least bit devastated. I was tempted to say *Are you INSANE?* Skye and Matt had been together for almost two years, so I'd met him at various gatherings and, let me tell you, I wouldn't dump him if he got herpes, drained my bank account, and stranded me alone with our unborn child. Not that I'm aspiring to be a disease-ridden, broke single mother, but Skye's ex- (oh my god, *ex*) boyfriend is the ideal male specimen. Matt is a tousled-hair prep-school boy, a multimillionaire with his own BMW and sailboat (seriously). And he's friendly, even to me. At Luce's Fourth of July barbeque last summer, Matt mentioned I should come on his boat sometime. Skye later joked that Matt invites the entire universe aboard his sailboat, but that didn't stop my ego from getting a serious boost.

The moms passed us on their way to coach.

"Hey, girls!" they called out.

As soon as they were gone, I turned to Skye. "So why did you break up with Matt?"

"I needed a change."

"How did he take it? Is he together with anyone else?"

Skye pursed her bee-stung lips. "Why are *you* so curious?"

"Whatever," I muttered, my cheeks flushing again.

Skye stuck in her earphones and settled her head on the pillow. Just before she closed her eyes, she said, "He's not exactly your type, Jena."

My stomach lurched. What she meant was I'm not *his* type. Duh. It's not like I don't know that.

As we taxied toward the runway, I sank back in my seat. I popped a few pieces of gum and opened *Dandelion Wine*. Skye looked like she was already asleep. The plane took off. I read a few chapters. I have no idea why my brother insisted I read this book, but it was all I had for the plane ride.

Once we reached cruising altitude, I double-checked that Skye was sleeping and then dug around for the Twix bar. I ripped open the paper and downed the whole thing, sucking the caramel out of my braces. As I stuffed the wrapper into my barf bag, I suddenly felt fat and gross. If I had any hope of landing a guy even *close* to Matt, I was now one Twix bar further from that happening.

four

There were a few minutes, when we first got to Paradise, that I thought maybe this trip was going to be okay after all. Maybe, deep down, I'm an optimist. Or maybe it was the sunlight and the lazily bending palm trees and the sweet scent of flowers in the air. I have this great Nicholas Sparks quote in my everything book. Something about how each day should be spent finding beauty in flowers and poetry and talking to animals. I doubted I'd be chatting up furry, four-legged creatures at Paradise, but I could definitely imagine beauty and poetry happening here.

As my mom parked the rental car, Luce checked us into the resort. Skye, who was queasy from the propeller plane we boarded in Puerto Rico and took to this island, disappeared into a bathroom. I sat on a wicker couch for a few minutes, waiting for Skye. When she didn't come out I decided to wander around.

The reception area had no walls, only a salmon-colored roof and a floor of smooth ceramic tiles. To the right of reception, I could see the tall windows of the gourmet restaurant Luce had been raving about. To the left, there were two white buildings with pink roofs, housing the guest suites. And outside, past the acres of manicured lawns, there was the Caribbean Sea. It was turquoise, sparkling, calm. I'd seen a few coastal areas in my life, Long Island and Myrtle Beach, but nothing compared to this. Not even close.

I was heading toward the water when Skye joined me. Her hair was pulled into a messy ponytail and she had one arm pressed across her stomach.

"Feeling okay?" I asked.

"I guess."

We meandered down a path lined with pink and yellow flowering bushes. Butterflies flitted around the lawn. We passed a pool and a gurgling hot tub tucked under a canopy of palm trees. A few middle-aged people were dozing on lounge chairs, fluffy white towels behind their heads.

The path ended at a beach. Skye and I kicked off our shoes and stepped onto the sand. There were more chairs lined up and some raised tent structures surrounded by gauzy curtains.

I'd changed into my shorts in the airport bathroom, but Skye still had her cargo pants on. As she bent over to roll up the cuffs, I stared out at the water. I could see a tiny red boat bobbing on the horizon.

"Jena?" Skye asked.

"Yeah?"

"I'm sorry about the Matt thing, from the airplane."

Skye was apologizing to *me*? I nearly doubled over in shock.

"Don't mind me on this trip, okay?" Skye dipped her toe into the water. "I'm going through some stuff."

Neither of us said anything. I was curious what Skye meant. What problems could she *possibly* have? But more than that, I couldn't get over the fact that Skye had apologized to me. Yes, it was bitchy to imply that Matt was out of my league. If Ellie or Leora said something like that, I'd change their friend status on ReaLife until they begged for forgiveness. But with Skye, I feel like I owe her a blanket apology just for *being*. For taking up space. I know Eleanor Roosevelt said "Nobody can make you feel inferior without your consent," but it's one thing to copy it into my everything book and it's another to actually believe it.

five

That night, at the restaurant, my mom and Luce did most of the talking. I was groggy because I ended up sleeping all afternoon. I hadn't meant to, but I lay down on one of the huge white beds in the huge airy room that Skye and I were sharing in the huge fancy suite that was our home for the next six days. The next thing I knew, Skye was returning from a workout at the health club and the moms were back from the beach and they were all taking showers and dressing for dinner and I was annoyed at myself because while everyone else was tanning or tightening, I was asleep. But that's how sleep happens for me. When I want it, it never comes. And when I'm not planning to pass out, I'm instantly comatose.

I was also quiet at dinner because I was feeling like an unstylish loser. My mom had said to pack casual so all

I had were T-shirts and shorts. *Wrong.* We were seated at an elegant table with cloth napkins and an artillery of spoons and forks and knives. There was a sweeping view of the sunset and it was one of those places where the waiters hustled around asking if everything was all right every time you buttered your bread.

And there I was, in my Old Navy shorts and orange flip-flops. Skye looked drop-dead elegant in a simple black sundress, silver jewelry, and low heels. Luce was wearing linen slacks and sandals. Even my mom had on a new skirt from the gift shop.

And to top it off, they were all drinking champagne. Even Skye.

I couldn't believe it when the waiter asked if I wanted some. He asked me first, so I thought he was joking. I actually chortled and said, "Ha! No! I'll have iced tea."

When he asked Skye, she nodded serenely and he filled her flute. But by that point, I couldn't take it back and say, *Oh, hey, I'm a big fat follower and I want some too.*

I guzzled my first glass of iced tea and they brought me another. Skye slowly sipped her drink. Luce talked about plans and how she thought we could hang out at Paradise tomorrow and explore the island the next day. Luce must be almost fifty, but she looks thirty. She's beautiful and petite and her blond hair is silky smooth. Skye's dad died before she was born, and my mom has told me that Luce has no interest in finding a husband. Not like she needs someone to support her. She owns an apartment in New York City and a house in the Hamptons, and they obviously have extra cash to fly first class to vacations like this.

The waiter came back to our table. My mom and Luce ordered the snapper and fried plantains. Skye got chicken salad with ginger-carrot dressing on the side. I was eyeing the creamy seafood risotto, but now that Skye ordered salad I couldn't exactly get a trough of fatty carbs. So when it was my turn I pretended to study the menu really hard in an attempt to look like I wasn't copying and then I ordered the chicken salad. Dressing on the side.

As we were eating, Luce asked my mom about my brother. Then my mom asked Skye about her acting and Skye and Luce began talking about Janet, Skye's manager. They all sipped their champagne. I downed a third class of iced tea.

Toward the end of dinner, I went to the bathroom. When I got back to the table, Skye was gone. Our dishes were cleared and my mom and Luce were glancing at the dessert menu.

"Where's Skye?" I asked, settling into my chair.

"She went back to the room," Luce said. "She's been working so hard recently. She's just exhausted."

"Is she getting over Matt?" my mom asked.

"You knew about Matt?" I asked.

My mom nodded.

"I think she is," Luce said. "He still calls her, but Skye says she doesn't want to get back together."

"How's homeschooling going?" my mom asked.

What? I wondered.

"Oh, fine," Luce said. "She's planning to take the GED exam this summer."

"Skye's not at Bentley anymore?" I asked. I was shocked. For our whole lives, Skye has gone to an elite private school called Bentley Prep. It's the kind of school you see in shows about girls who wear teensy pleated skirts, toddle around in thousand-dollar heels, and have legs that, miraculously, never need shaving. Not that I've ever visited Bentley, but I've looked at the pictures online.

"She wanted to have more flexibility," Luce said to me. "More time to concentrate on her career."

As my mom and Luce drained their champagne flutes, I wondered what it must be like to be seventeen and have a *career*. The only work I have is my Saturday night babysitting gig where I watch princess movies with the four-year-old girl and, no matter how carefully I fasten the baby's diaper, he always ends up peeing on my leg.

That first night, as everyone else was sleeping, I lay awake in my bed. Of course I was awake. I slept all afternoon and drank four glasses of caffeinated iced tea. Brilliant move, Jena.

Skye was asleep, so I turned on my light and opened *Dandelion Wine*. I was at this part where a guy, Leo, decides to build a Happiness Machine that'll make people delighted to be alive. I slipped my everything book off the bedside table and jotted down *Happiness Machine*. I tried to picture what I'd have in my Happiness Machine. A boyfriend? Definitely. But not like Leora's boyfriend, who laughs when he burps and acts like his farts are a gift from God. I want someone mature and kind, someone who loves me for who I am.

Of course, by chapter thirteen, Leo's Happiness Machine goes bust and anyone who sits in it weeps uncontrollably. Perfect. I set *Dandelion Wine* back on my bedside table, tiptoed into the bathroom, and stared at my reflection in the mirror. Was there any speck of hope I'd meet a guy on this vacation? I tried to assess the likelihood that I'd be swept into an embrace on one of these soft, sandy Caribbean beaches. From far away, I'm shortish and curvy with shoulder-length brown hair and okay-sized boobs. But step closer and I've got dimpled thighs, braces, and this recent crop of zits on my chin. Definitely nothing luscious going on here.

I wriggled a bra under my shirt, slid my feet into my flip-flops, and crept past my mom and Luce, sleeping quietly in their queen beds. I closed the door behind me, and headed down the corridor and onto the hushed lawn.

The grounds were dark except for the light from the moon, which hung, suspended, over the sea. I walked past the surf shop, past the wooden dock, and across the beach. The only sounds I could hear were the waves slapping against the shore.

I know I was at Paradise and it was supposed to be, well, paradise, but in reality I felt lonely. I longed to be home, nestled on the couch, laughing my butt off with Ellie and Leora, or noshing the cupboards bare with Grandma Belle in Binghamton. As it was, I didn't even get phone reception on this island, so I couldn't call my friends, couldn't send one measly text.

I brushed the sand off my feet and wandered past the pool and the hot tub, toward the business center. The bellhop who carried our luggage mentioned they have wireless in there. It's open twenty-four hours, so I decided to pop in and say hi to my girls. It was after midnight, but they'd probably be online, at least Ellie, who shares my predisposition toward insomnia.

There was one other person in the business center—a guy around my age, tall and thin with reddish-blondish hair. He was wearing earphones and staring at a laptop that was plastered with bumper stickers. I settled at a computer, logged on, and began chatting with Ellie. At first she was sympathetic to my plight, but then she reminded me that it's forty-one degrees, driving rain, and utterly boring back in Topeka. As we chatted, I kept glancing over at the guy, his fingers moving furiously across the keyboard. I wondered who he was talking with. Probably his girlfriend, a funky chick who dyes her hair pink and plays in a garage band on weekends. I bet he was telling her he couldn't wait to see her again. I wondered if a guy would ever write those kinds of things to me.

After a few minutes, Ellie said she had to attempt sleep. I wished her luck. Once we logged off, I went onto my favorite quote-of-the-day site, but they'd posted an overused Pablo Neruda line. Boring.

I stood up. The guy next to me was still pounding at his computer. Since I'm a total snoop, I walked by very slowly, trying to glimpse what he was writing. He had his music on and his eyes were intent on the screen, so I paused stealthily behind him. There were a lot of photos and wordy paragraphs. I stepped closer and realized it was a blog. I could even see the name: Loser with a Laptop.

Loser with a Laptop?

No way. Sure this guy was skinny, but he had a cute face and supercool hair. Plus, a bumper sticker on his laptop proclaimed: A DAY WITHOUT SUNSHINE IS, LIKE, NIGHT, which I've always thought is one of the funniest ever.

I remained there for another second, staring at the back of his head. What would happen if I tapped his shoulder and said, "Hey, I'm Jena. Sometimes I feel like a loser too. How would you like to close your computer and have a conversation with me because maybe, if you put two losers together, we'd actually have a shot."

But that's not how life works. So I pushed through the door, padded across the dark lawn, and crawled into bed.

ʃix

Paradise was sucking.

Have I mentioned that a deranged flock of roosters began cock-a-doodle-doing at six every morning? Also, Skye was barely talking to me. She just slept and watched shows on her iPhone and worked out at the health club and slathered her body in sunblock only to take a dip in the pool and then dodge into the shade again. That was a major topic of conversation between Skye and Luce: lamenting Skye's tendency to tan quickly because of her half-Brazilian heritage, making sure Skye's skin was the right shade for her auditions next week, calling Skye's manager in New York to double-check the appropriate skin color for those auditions.

It wasn't that Skye was being bitchy. Mostly, she was distant, like I didn't exist. I wondered if she was mad we'd crashed her vacation. Or maybe she just thought I was a lost cause, not worth wasting her breath on. That's how it felt one afternoon when I was playing solitaire on the balcony and she came out to hang a towel on the railing.

"Want to play?" I asked.

"Cards?" she asked in this voice that implied I was suggesting Go Fish.

I held up an ace of hearts. They were typical cards with a red lattice design, not plastered with kittens or anything. "Yeah . . . maybe Spit or rummy?"

Skye shook her head and went back inside.

So that was the gist of Paradise. Solitaire all the way. The moms were always playing tennis or walking on the beach or visiting the spa. Luce suggested I get a massage and charge it to the room, but she was treating us to everything so I felt weird having her pay for that, too. Instead I visited the book exchange, where I swapped *Dandelion Wine* for a water-stained copy of *The Bridges of Madison County*, which I vaguely remember Grandma Belle sobbing into a few years ago.

Oh, and speaking of the trip sucking, I can't forget to mention Skye's bikini. But first, there was mine. I'd ordered a tankini from Lands' End, hoping it would be slimming. But instead of the "rich brown" they'd promised, the color ended up more on the fecal spectrum. Also, I assumed the style would be flattering, but the bottoms stretched wide over my hips and the top had this annoying habit of sliding up, revealing my untoned tummy.

Which brings me back to Skye.

That first morning at Paradise, Luce made reservations for us to take a ferry out to another island a few minutes away. It leaves from the resort every hour, and people at breakfast kept saying how amazing the island is, an uninhabited sandbar out in the ocean.

The ride across the bay was quick, maybe five or ten minutes. Once we got to the island, we trekked down a path that ended at a secluded beach enveloped by palm trees. My mom and Luce spread out their towels and stripped down to their swimsuits. Skye wriggled her cotton dress over her head and hung it on a branch. She and Luce had a brief consultation about sunblock and how much time Skye should spend in the sun. As everyone started toward the water, I slunk under a tree.

"Jena?" my mom called. "Aren't you coming in?"

I burrowed my toes in the sand. "I'm not that hot."

"The water's great!" Luce shouted.

"Maybe after I warm up," I muttered.

I was plenty warm. In fact, sweat was festering in my cleavage. But there was no way I could expose my body. Not now. Not in front of Skye.

She was perfect. Even more perfect than with her clothes on. She had those big boobs and a flat stomach and narrow hips and long legs and everything was amazingly toned. Also, her snow-white bikini was the kind you see celebrities wearing, with the tiny triangle tops and teensy string bottoms.

I watched Skye splash in the water and I thought about how unfair it is that one person is endowed with so many gifts. I bet she's even had sex. She was with Matt for almost two years. And there's no way someone could have that body and wear that bikini and *not* be a sex goddess.

The only bright spot at Paradise was that there was a hot guy on the premises.

I first saw him on Sunday afternoon, our second day here. Skye and her flat stomach were safely confined in the health club, so I decided to take a dip in the pool. But on my way I stopped in my tracks. There, perched on the diving board, was a hot, muscular, shirtless (did I mention hot?) guy. He had sinewy arms and a six-pack stomach. He looked like he was eighteen or nineteen, with curly brown hair, a tanned chest, and one of those surfer-style seashell necklaces.

As I gawked, he turned around, stretched his arms over his head, and did a backward dive. When he didn't come up for several seconds, I panicked that he'd smacked his head on the bottom of the pool. *Great.* Just when I encountered the man of my dreams, he had to go unconscious on me.

I was trying to recall the specifics of that CPR unit from health class when he popped up on the other side. Here was my chance! I sucked in my gut and strutted past the pool, hoping he'd check me out. Once I was several strides away, I peeked over my shoulder, thinking how we could make long, meaningful eye contact, the start of our love affair.

But no. He was swimming underwater, oblivious.

Even so, I spent the next day and a half scheming about how I could talk to him. The biggest thing working for me was that, other than Skye (who wasn't talking to anyone), there were no other girls at Paradise.

Finally, on Tuesday, I saw him again. I was walking over to the grill to order nachos and I glanced toward the parking lot. There he was, opening the passenger door of a white car. A middle-aged woman was in the driver's seat, probably his mom. Right before he climbed in, he stretched his arms over his head (oh my god), which made his shirt lift up (oh my god), and, with his shorts riding low (oh my god), I got a glimpse of an amazing V-cut leading down to his you-know-where (total visual orgasm).

I veered into the parking lot and began racing through the rows of shiny rental cars. It's almost like a force beyond my control was pulling me toward him. But just as I approached, he got into the car, slammed the door, and they sped off.

seven

Late that night, I was wide awake as usual. My mom, Luce, and I went to a phosphorescent bay earlier in the evening. It was a half-hour drive from here. Once it got dark, we rode out on a boat to see sparkling plankton. My mom spent the whole time gushing about how amazing it is and we never would have been able to do this on our own and thank you, Luce, for bringing us along. The phosphorescent stuff *was* amazing, but I was relieved Skye wasn't here to witness my mom's big display. Just as we were leaving for the bay, Skye bailed. She'd announced that she was ordering room service and going to bed early. For the whole drive Luce talked about Skye's draining auditions, but I kept remembering what she said to me, about how she's going through some stuff.

When we got back to the room, Skye was asleep. I read the last seventy pages of *The Bridges of Madison County* in one hungry gulp. It's a love story between two middle-aged people that doesn't sound high on the sexy scale. But believe me, it was. Especially this one line that the guy, Robert, says to the woman, Francesca. It's the last night they're spending together and they've pretty much realized they're going to have to go their separate ways after this. They're laying in bed and he whispers, "In a universe of ambiguity, this kind of certainty comes only once, and never again, no matter how many lifetimes you live." I wrote that in my everything book, and then cried into my pillow for five minutes straight.

Around eleven thirty, I crawled out of bed. Other nights here, when I couldn't sleep, I walked around the resort or chatted online with Ellie and Leora. Tonight, though, I wasn't in a wandering mood. All I could think about was Robert and Francesca and whether that certainty will ever come my way (and, if so, please give me the time, date, and location). I needed something to calm me down. Maybe a soak in the hot tub. It was late, after all. No one around to see me in my poop-tankini glory.

I tiptoed to the bathroom and changed into my

bathing suit. I wrapped a white towel around myself, and crept out the door and down the stairs.

The hot tub was steaming and there was only the dimmest light from the pool area. I tossed my towel on a chair, hit the button for the bubbles, and lowered myself in. As the warmth washed over my body, I stirred my legs around in the water. Maybe I could be like Francesca, full of untapped lust, waiting for the man of my dreams to pull into my driveway in his old pickup truck.

I'd just closed my eyes when a voice said, "How's the temp?"

I looked up and my heart plummeted, I swear, into my colon. Because there, standing above me and ripping off his shirt, was the guy. The guy from the diving board. The guy with the muscular calves and, oh god, the swimsuit riding low enough for me to conjure up some serious imagery.

"It's fine," I muttered. Then I sank even deeper into the water.

This was *not* how it was supposed to happen. I was supposed to bump into him when I was clothed, my hair blown out, makeup on. I know some girls, like Skye, can pull off the *au naturel* thing. But I need all the intervention the cosmetic world has to offer.

As he climbed into the tub, I had a sudden panic that I was going to fart and even though the light was faint he'd detect telltale bubbles. I quickly reassured myself that the jets were on (good move, Jena), so I was covered on one front. But that still left me in a hot tub, barely clothed, with the hottest guy on the planet.

It doesn't get more awful than this.

I planted my ankles firmly on the ground so I wouldn't knock into him and he wouldn't think I was flirting and run screaming across Paradise, laughing at the notion that someone like me would think I had a shot with someone like him.

But I could still gawk, right?

And so, with my face angled toward the gurgling water, I watched this guy settle his body in the water (oh), groan slightly (my), fold his arms behind his head (freaking), and close his eyes (god!).

Since his eyes were shut, I took this opportunity to slide as far as possible to the other side of the hot tub. Once there, I stretched my arms behind myself in an attempt to appear relaxed.

And that's when I felt it.

My fingers had landed on a folded-up piece of paper sitting on the edge of the hot tub. I stared at it for a moment, debating between two competing impulses.

Impulse #1: My self-preserving instinct to remain as motionless as possible.

Impulse #2: My obsessive need to read the contents of any discarded note.

Obsession beat out self-preservation. I opened the paper, careful not to ruin the ink with my damp fingers. There was just enough light for me to squint at the small, loopy letters. But once I began reading, a horrible, sick feeling washed over me.

Oh my god, I thought.

"What?" the guy asked.

I looked at him. Had I said that out loud?

"Oh my god *what*?" the guy pressed.

I shook my head and gestured at the paper I was pinching between my fingers. My throat was tight as I whispered, "I just found this right there."

He paddled across the tub, slid in next to me, and glanced at the note. I reread it along with him.

> I keep thinking about slicing my wrists. I wonder if I could really do it? I can imagine the open wounds, but I don't feel any pain. I just close my eyes and the blood soaks the clean white sheets and I finally feel free.

The guy let out a low whistle. "Holy shit."

"I know," I said quietly.

"Holy shit," he said again. "You just found this?"

"Yeah."

"Where?"

"Right there."

Neither of us spoke. He was squinching his eyes shut and massaging his temples with his fingers. I was now fluctuating between two competing emotions.

Emotion #1: To be utterly freaked out, bad-variety. After all, I was holding a suicide note in my hand.

Emotion #2: To be utterly freaked out, good-variety. After all, the hottest guy in the planet was sitting next to me. His thigh had brushed against mine ever so briefly, and the tickle of his leg hair had plunged my brain into a complete state of freeze.

I forced myself to muddle through the mental tundra. "Do you think we should do something about it?" I asked.

"Like what?" He glanced at me. "Tell housekeeping to watch out for their clean white sheets? Remove sharp objects from the kitchen?"

I swallowed hard, wishing I hadn't said anything in the first place.

"I'm just saying," the guy added, "that whoever

wrote that note is a fucking idiot. If you want to die, go ahead and kill yourself. I'm not going to stop you. But it's insane to take your own life. I mean, you never know when your time is up so why do it yourself?"

I studied him, unsure how to even *begin* responding when he jumped out of the tub, jogged over to a table, and grabbed a beer from under his T-shirt. Then he slid back into the water and tilted the can into his mouth. After a long chug, he set the beer on the edge, wiped his lips, and said, "It sucks, okay? But it's not our problem. Let's start again. I'm Dakota. I'm from upstate New York. Who're you?"

Dakota. His name was Dakota.

"I'm—I'm Jena," I stumbled. My brain was darting all over the place. This guy—Dakota—was starting a conversation with me (wow). But I was currently in possession of a note written by someone who was about to slit their wrists (even bigger wow). Or maybe Dakota was the bigger wow? But if someone killed—

"You're cute, you know that?" Dakota added. "In a shy way. I like that. Where're you from?"

That did it. I set the paper on the edge of the tub and swirled my hands around in the hot water. "Topeka," I said.

"Kansas?"

41

"No, the one in Westchester County, north of New York City."

He studied me, but didn't say anything. And so I, immediately, went into hyperkinetic babble mode.

"People don't realize this," I added, "but there are also Topekas in Indiana, Illinois, and Mississippi. Supposedly *Topeka* is a Native American expression that means 'to dig good potatoes.' Great, right? Some people live in the entertainment capital of the world and I live in a place where you can dig good potatoes."

"You sure have a lot to say about Topeka," he remarked, his lip curled in a lopsided grin.

I flushed. I am *such* a moron. I tried to imagine Skye here instead of me. She would definitely not be talking about potatoes. Then again, she's the kind of girl who could recite a monologue on root vegetables and still have him begging for more.

Dakota took another swig of beer. "So what do you think of Paradise?"

I shrugged. I wasn't going to say another word for the rest of my life. Not one.

"I'm here with my mom and brother," he continued, "so it's kind of boring."

Oh my god! There were *two* of them? I couldn't help myself. "You have a brother?"

"Yeah, but you can barely tell," Dakota said. "He's younger than me, but he's really tall and has reddish hair. You probably haven't seen him. All he does is hang out in that business center."

I was incredulous. "The *Loser with the Laptop* guy is your *brother*?"

Dakota laughed. "That's one name for him."

I was starting to feel light-headed from the heat, but there was no way I was going to climb out in front of him. Not in this tankini. Not with these thighs.

"How old are you?" Dakota asked.

"Sixteen. How about you?"

"Eighteen."

As I rested my head against the side of the tub, Dakota told me that his mom brought his brother and him here in an attempt to bond, but they haven't been spending any time together. Mostly, Dakota's been sleeping late (that body in a *bed* . . . sigh), scoring beer from the bar, and swimming out in search of fierce currents.

"In the ocean?" I asked, lifting my head up.

"No, in the pool." Dakota laughed. "Yeah, in the ocean. It's pretty cool, almost like you're losing control. But once you hit undertow you have to float for a while until you can swim back to the shallow water."

"That reminds me of this line from an Edie Brickell song. 'Choke me in the shallow water before I get too deep.'"

"Who's Edie Brickell?"

I shrugged. "A singer. She's not new or anything."

"Haven't heard of her." Dakota drained the rest of his beer. Then he hoisted himself out of the tub and tossed his can in the trash.

I watched as he pulled on his shirt and combed his fingers through his hair. But then, just as I was expecting him to leave, he reached for my towel and held it out. *Oh, no,* I thought, shrinking into the water.

"Come on," Dakota said. "I'll dry you off."

"That's okay," I squeaked. "I mean, I'm fine. I think I'll stay in for a few more minutes."

Total lie. If I soaked any longer I'd die of heatstroke.

"No, seriously," he said. "Now you're getting all shy again."

I climbed out of the tub, gripping the rail to steady myself, and dove into the outstretched towel. Dakota wrapped it around me (phew), but then, as he was tucking in the front, his hand lingered on my boob area.

My legs went jelly on me. I leaned into him for support. He stepped in closer too, reached his arm around my waist, and touched my chin with his thumb, gently pulling my face up.

"You're cute, Jena from Topeka," he whispered.

My teeth began clacking inside my skull. Was this happening? Was this happening? Was this really—

Dakota kissed me. It was soft at first, but then his lips pushed harder against mine and his tongue darted into my mouth. It all transpired so quickly I didn't even have a chance to worry about whether my braces were butchering his flesh.

Dakota stepped back, grinning. "See you around, okay?"

I nodded, unable to speak. He headed across the lawn. As I watched him disappear into the darkness, I held my towel tight to my chest. I was grinning and my teeth were chattering and I kept thinking, *No way. No way. Oh my god. Yes way.* I must have stood there, smiling and repeating that in my head, for five minutes. But that's the good thing about being an insomniac. You're up so late there's no one around to witness your crazier moments. And even if there were, I was flying way too high to care.

eight

The next morning, the roosters woke me at six. I stretched across my bed in disbelief. Did I *really* meet that guy in the hot tub last night and did he *really* say I was cute and did he *really* wrap me in a towel and kiss me so passionately it was like I'd stepped out of my life and into a romance novel?

No, I kept telling myself. *That's too good to be true. There's no way it could have happened.*

But it did.

I knew it did.

I don't generally believe in heaven. But as I lay there reliving last night's encounter, I was *so* up there.

Breakfast takes place in a large open-air space that doubles as a grill for lunch and a bar in the nighttime.

On Wednesday morning, as I navigated the buffet line, I kept looking for Dakota. My mom was in front of me, ladling syrup onto her French toast. Skye was behind me, picking through the fruit selection. I was trying not to be obvious, but I wanted to see him so badly I couldn't even think about food. I took some mango slices and a small container of yogurt, but ate only a few bites.

Near the end of the meal, I was back in the buffet line getting juice for my mom when a voice behind me said, "Hey there."

It was Dakota, freshly showered, wearing khaki shorts, a T-shirt, and that seashell necklace. He looked every bit as gorgeous as I'd remembered.

"How's it going?" he asked.

"Okay," I mumbled, nearly dropping the glass.

"What are you up to today?"

"Just hanging out. What about you?"

Dakota rolled his eyes. "My mom wants to hike to a lighthouse on the other side of the island. We probably won't get back until tonight."

"Oh," I said. (*Damn*, I thought.)

"Want to meet up later? Down at the beach?"

DID I WANT TO MEET UP LATER??!!!!!

"Uh . . . sure."

"What's your number?" Dakota pulled out his phone. "I'll text you when I get back."

HE WANTED TO TEXT ME!!!!!

"Number?" Dakota asked.

I had to pull myself together. "I don't get reception here," I said.

"Want me to call your room then?"

I thought about what would happen if Dakota called our room and Skye answered and ended up joining us on the beach. No way was I getting myself in a situation where he had his pick of her or me.

"That's okay," I said quickly. "I'll just hang out down there until you show up."

"Let's meet around ten," Dakota said. Then he leaned toward me and whispered, "I'll get us some beer."

"Who were you talking to in the buffet line?" Skye asked as we were walking back to the suite. The moms were ahead of us, harmonizing some song. They were in an a cappella group in college. Whenever they get together, they invariably break out in a bouncy bop-bop-de-bop tune.

"Some guy." I shrugged. "He's here with his mom and brother."

"You seemed pretty friendly," she murmured.

"It's no big deal."

"He looks kind of suburban, doesn't he?"

"I don't think so," I said defensively. Honestly, I wasn't even sure what she meant. But given that I'm not all New York City cool like Skye, I most likely fit into that category as well.

"Did you see that necklace he was wearing?" Skye asked. "Does he think he's Hawaiian?" Then she shook her head and added, "Do whatever you want, but don't say I didn't warn you."

All I could think about the whole day was Dakota, our amazing kiss, meeting him on the beach tonight. Now and then, my thoughts drifted to the suicide note. I'd reread it in the morning and even taped it into my everything book. I'd contemplated showing my mom, or maybe Skye, but then I decided that Dakota was right. At the end of the day there was nothing we could do to stop this person.

That night, when my mom and Luce went to the bar for a drink, I washed my hair and shaved my legs. After I toweled off, I borrowed a squirt of Skye's expensive lavender moisturizer. Then I got worried she'd smell it, so I lifted my shins into the sink, scrubbed them off, and rubbed on my cheap stuff.

A little before ten, I came out of the bathroom. Skye was sitting cross-legged on her bed, watching TV.

"I'm going for a walk," I said casually.

Skye studied my sarong (purchased from the gift shop earlier today with all my babysitting money) and my mom's low-cut top (stolen from her closet). She raised her eyebrows and said, "Be careful."

There was no one at the beach, just a row of empty lounge chairs. It was darker than up by the pool and cool, with the breeze off the water. I hugged my arms around my chest. I could hear laughing from the bar area. I wondered if Dakota was scoring us those beers.

When Dakota didn't show after fifteen minutes, I crept up the lawn, past the pool, all the way to the edge of the bar. I could see my mom and Luce at a table in the far corner. Luce was tracing her finger around the edge of her glass. My mom was drinking from a pineapple. No sign of Dakota, though. I hurried back down to the beach.

I sagged into a lounge chair and looked up at the palm trees and the starry sky. Dakota stood me up. He totally stood me up. He saw me at breakfast and decided he didn't like the looks of me in the daylight.

"Hey, sleepyhead," a voice said.

I opened my eyes. I must have drifted off. Dakota was standing above me, a silver can in each hand and one jammed in each pocket, too.

"Sorry it took so long," he said as he settled onto the chair next to mine. "My mom got lost on the drive back and I kept saying she should let me take the wheel but she said no because it's a rental car and we got into this argument and—" Dakota cracked open a beer. "Let's just say I could really use this right now."

I was doing everything in my power not to fling myself into his arms and thank him for showing up.

"Want one?" He held up a beer for me.

I took a small taste (disgusting) and attempted not to wince (*seriously* disgusting). Dakota raised his drink to his lips and took a long swig.

"Cheers," he said, clinking cans with me. "Here's to stupid lighthouses."

"To stupid lighthouses," I chimed.

There was a brief silence. I scanned my brain for something to say.

"Are you in college?" I asked.

"Next year. I'm going to Fredonia. I can't wait to graduate and get the hell out of high school."

"You don't like your high school?"

"I like wrestling and baseball okay, but I don't think

51

anyone actually *likes* high school. Why . . . do you?"

I was still processing the fact that I was on the beach with a guy who does wrestling and baseball (jocks *never, ever* talk to me at Topeka High) when Dakota said, "I bet you like school, right?"

I sipped my beer (still disgusting). "I didn't say that."

"I can tell. You're one of those smart chicks who raises her hand all the time and the guys secretly want to fuck you and live out their librarian fantasies."

I can honestly say that the guys at my school do *not* want to do that, but I wasn't about to tell Dakota. Let him think I'm in high demand. Let him think he's landed a brainiac by day, sexpot by night (ha).

After another silence, I said, "I didn't find any more suicide notes today."

Dakota looked out at the water but didn't say anything.

"I still wonder who wrote it," I added.

"Could have been any person here. You never know how miserable people really are, even if they look happy on the surface."

I thought about this Thoreau line I had in my everything book. "Most men lead lives of quiet desperation." I considered mentioning it to Dakota, but after his librarian comment I opted to keep quiet.

"We should go skinny-dipping," Dakota said, nodding toward the ocean.

I gaped at him. Was he seriously suggesting we strip off our clothes and go swimming? No way. Besides, if Dakota saw me naked he'd hardly call it *skinny-*dipping.

"I didn't think so," Dakota said, reading my expression. Then he gestured to one of the raised tent structures. It was almost like a loft bed, with a mattress and everything, except it was enveloped by yards of gauzy fabric. "At least let's go in there. It's fucking cold down here."

Dakota opened a second beer, pulled back the curtain, and climbed inside. I set my can in the sand and followed him in. As I arranged my sarong over my knees, Dakota balanced his beer on the wooden frame.

"Just so you know," he said, grinning, "you have some fine-looking tits."

I nearly gagged on my tongue. But before I could recover, Dakota began kissing me. His mouth was cold from the beer. As we were making out, his fingers wandered up my back and expertly unhooked my bra, faster than I could do it myself. He'd just started feeling me up (oh my god, a guy was *feeling me up*) when he took one of my hands and pulled it down (oh, no) between his legs. The next thing I knew, Dakota was unzipping his shorts (oh, no) and pushing my hand (oh, no, no, no) inside the elastic band of his boxers.

And there it was, pressing against my wrist. *His boner.* It was warm and firm and pulsing a little. And there was all this hair, much more than I thought a guy would have.

I was in complete panic mode. My ears were swishing and I was having a hard time catching my breath. It's not like I wanted Dakota to be a Ken doll (all hotness, no penis), but this was moving WAY too fast.

I wriggled my hand out of his boxers.

"Something wrong?" Dakota asked.

"It's just . . ." I yanked my shirt back down around my stomach. "I just . . . I don't even know your last name."

"Evans," Dakota said quickly.

"Oh."

Dakota sighed. "I guess it sucks for me tonight."

"I'm sorry," I whispered, swallowing back tears.

"I'm kidding." Dakota grinned as he drank some beer. "But maybe you'll at least consider letting me feel you up some more."

I thought he was joking, so I lay there quietly, unsure what to do. But then Dakota walked his fingers across my belly and eased my shirt back up again.

nine

The next morning, Luce insisted we visit this beach famous for its clear water and sugary white sand. I overheard Skye telling her mom that she'd rather stay at the resort, that she'd get carsick on the winding roads. Honestly, I was hoping to stay back, too, but it was our last full day so Luce declared it a mandatory outing.

We left Paradise after breakfast and stopped in a nearby grocery store to load up on picnic supplies. As my mom and Luce cruised the aisles, Skye and I stood near the front. Skye was staring at a Spanish soap opera on a TV mounted from the ceiling. I was leaning against the wall, blinking back sleep.

I didn't go to bed last night until two twenty. Dakota and I had fooled around in that tent and then we just lay there listening to the ocean. The next thing I knew he was asleep. I stayed still for the longest time, watching him. His lips were parted, his arms slung by his sides. I couldn't help wondering how many other girls have laid next to him like this. Dozens, I bet. Then I started obsessing about how Dakota is eighteen and maybe I should have given him that handjob after all and how I probably came across as totally inexperienced. What did I think a gorgeous eighteen-year-old guy was going to expect? An Eskimo kiss?

"You got in late last night," Skye said.

I glanced at her. The soap opera had broken for a commercial and she was examining one of her manicured fingernails.

"I guess," I said.

"Were you with that suburban guy?"

"He's from a small town," I said. "Not a suburb."

"What's up with you two?"

"We were just hanging out," I said.

Skye shook her head.

"What?" I asked.

"Nothing," Skye said, looking up at the television again.

When we piled back in the car, Skye climbed into the front seat. My mom was in the rear next to me. Almost immediately, she and Luce launched into a sing-along. I rested my head against the window and closed my eyes. By the time we got to the beach, the sun was high in the sky. Luce parked the car under a grove of palm trees. I slid my feet into my flip-flops and we all grabbed our stuff and trekked toward the water.

My mom and Luce lay some towels under a sprawling Tamarind tree. Skye dove into the shade. As she plugged in her earphones and the moms meandered down the beach in search of shells, I stared at the clear turquoise bay.

I wanted to go in so badly.

(But there's no way I could strip down in front of Skye.)

When would I get another chance to swim in calm Caribbean water?

(But how could I deal with the humiliation of Skye seeing my body? I'd been so careful all week, changing in the bathroom, wearing long T-shirts and boxers to bed.)

Then I reminded myself of Dakota. I thought about how much he'd swooned over my boobs. He basically didn't take his hands off them the whole time we were kissing. And I wondered if maybe I'm not so bad after all. Maybe I'm actually a little bit luscious, like

Grandma Belle says.

Luscious, I thought. That's what I'll be. Not perfect. Not flawless. Luscious.

I pulled up my shirt, kicked off my shorts, and jogged across the beach in my tankini. As I splashed into the salty water, I thought about what Dakota had told me that first night, how he liked to venture out in search of dangerous currents. My whole life, I've always picked the safe route, but maybe that's starting to change. Maybe since meeting Dakota I've realized I need to live more, take more risks.

I swam farther out and then turned onto my back. My body sank into the water. I took a deep breath, held it in my lungs, and floated to the surface again. The sun was fierce on my cheeks. The water was lapping around my ears. I exhaled, took another breath, and stared up at the sky.

After a while, I did a mermaid dive and plunged as far into the water as I could go. When I bobbed up again, gasping for air, I thought, *Let this be the start of a whole new Jena.*

When we got back to Paradise, my mom and Luce left for their spa appointments. I wrapped my new sarong over my tankini and grabbed my cards. As I headed down to the beach, I could feel myself walking differently, a little sway to my hips.

Skye was stretched on a lounge chair in the shade, watching a show on her iPhone. With her oversized sunglasses and her hair twisted up, she looked every bit the glamorous movie star. Yesterday, I would have screeched on the brakes, U-turned, and parked at the pool area instead. But not the new me, with my top riding lusciously low, my skin clearing up from the sun, finally a little tan going on. The new me sat on the chair next to Skye and began shuffling my cards.

A few minutes later, Dakota tapped my shoulder.

"Hey!" I said. I couldn't help it, but my pulse raced at the sight of him and I got an instant smile on my face.

"I thought I saw you coming down here. What's up?"

"Not much." *Sound relaxed*, I instructed myself. *Be the new me*. "We just got back a little while ago."

Dakota glanced over at Skye.

"Oh, this is Skye," I said as casually as possible. "Skye, this is Dakota."

Dakota nodded his chin in Skye's direction. Skye said hi back to him.

"Listen," Dakota said to me. "I'm about to take that

ferry out to the island. Want to come?"

I glanced toward the dock, where the water taxi was throwing its rope. There was a family getting on and a guy already sitting inside.

"Seriously?" I asked. "Right now?"

"Come on, babe," Dakota said. "It's not like I'm asking you to elope. It's only for an hour. The ferry comes back at five."

Skye giggled, and she and Dakota exchanged a brief glance. But the new me wasn't going to obsess. Besides, he'd called me *babe*. How can anyone say no to babe?

I turned to Skye. "Can you watch my stuff?"

"Sure," Skye said without looking up.

Dakota and I dashed toward the dock. We arrived just as the captain was unhooking the rope. He muttered something to us in Spanish and rubbed his stubby fingers against his thumb. As Dakota pulled out some dollars, I said, "Oh, no!"

"What?" Dakota asked.

"I don't have any money with me."

"Don't worry about it." Dakota handed some more bills to the guy, leaped into the boat, and reached for my hand.

As I climbed in next to him, I was smiling so hard.

Dakota bought my ticket! Not only was he whisking me to a tropical island, he was paying my way, too.

The ferry puttered into the bay. The captain was at the front, with the other people sitting directly behind him. That left Dakota and me by ourselves in the back row. I glanced over at him, wondering if we'd find a deserted spot on the island, maybe fool around. If things heated up, I wouldn't freak out this time. I'd actually stopped by the business center and begged Ellie and Leora for advice. Leora instructed me to practice by getting a banana, holding it tightly, and running my fingers back and forth. I didn't feel like sexually stimulating a piece of fruit, but I told her I got the point.

"I'm going to jump off," Dakota said to me.

I turned to Dakota, startled out of my tropical-island hookup fantasy.

"You're *what*?" I asked. The wind was stronger out here so I wasn't even sure I'd heard him correctly.

Dakota ran his fingers along his seashell necklace. "I'm going to jump off, see if I can swim the rest of the way to the island."

I stared in disbelief. It was rough out here, choppy waves rising in every direction. Not to mention that there had to be sharks in these waters.

"It'll be fine," Dakota said. "If I can't make it, I'll just swim back to shore."

Before I could say anything else, Dakota scaled the back railing and slid into the water. His head went under for a second and I could feel a scream erupting from the back of my throat. I wanted to shout for the captain to stop the boat or throw him a life preserver, but I knew I couldn't. If I busted Dakota, he'd never talk to me again. Besides, the new me was cooler than that (even if it made me die of an anxiety attack).

And so I watched, my heart pounding, as Dakota swam behind the boat. The waves were slapping into his face and his expression was strained. *Please keep swimming*, I willed him as the ferry pulled farther and farther ahead. *Please be okay.*

We rounded the corner and I couldn't see Dakota anymore. Even so, I kept glancing back at the water. The ferry docked at the island. As I made my way to the front, the captain grabbed me.

"*¿Dónde está ese muchacho?*" he barked.

I knew he was talking about Dakota but I shook my head as if I didn't understand. Then I wriggled away from him, rubbing my arm where he'd squeezed me, and hopped onto the land. I could see the captain staring nervously into the ocean.

I wandered down the path and settled on a stretch of beach that faced Paradise. I could hear people laughing and shrieking in the surf, but I didn't move. I just looked out at the water, worried Dakota wasn't showing up, worried he'd drowned. Maybe it's selfish, but I also felt disappointed. I'd been hoping we'd wander around this island together. And here I was, no guy in sight. As usual.

The ferry circled the bay, stopping at various docks. After an hour or so, it pulled up to the island again. By this time, I had to assume Dakota had swum back to the hotel. I brushed the sand off my butt and made my way to the boat. When I passed the captain, I avoided any eye contact. My arm was still hurting from where he'd grabbed me.

The ferry rounded the bend. I could see Paradise in the distance, the green lawns, the long pool shimmering in the afternoon light. There were the raised tents, the beach, the narrow dock. As we got closer, I spotted Skye in her lounge chair just like before and then—

Dakota was sitting in the chair next to hers.

I got a horrible feeling in my stomach. As the captain threw the rope over the cleat, I sat there for a moment, not wanting to move.

Somehow I made it off the boat. Somehow I walked down the dock, across the sand, and over to where

Skye and Dakota were playing gin rummy. With my cards.

"Hey!" Skye said, smiling at me like we were best friends.

I didn't say anything.

Dakota glanced up. "The current was too intense. I had to turn around."

Skye grabbed the deck away from Dakota. "My deal!"

"No way, bitch!" Dakota said, reaching over and tickling her perfect belly.

I stood there, waiting. I'm not sure what for. Maybe for them to invite me to play cards with them, or to say they were just joking, that Dakota was still mine and Skye still didn't care about talking to anyone. But neither of them said a word. My tankini was giving me a wedgie and my new sarong was too clingy and even though an hour ago I thought I was a luscious babe, I suddenly felt chunky and stupid.

"I'm going to take a shower," I said quietly.

"Oh, okay," Dakota said, barely glancing up.

I walked slowly to the room. When I got there, I collapsed facedown on the bed, my swimsuit still damp, my feet still crusted with sand.

ten

At first, I cried. Then I dozed off. Once I woke up, I started crying again.

I couldn't believe Skye had stolen Dakota from me. She knew we were hanging out. Plus, all she could say about him was that he was too suburban. And who could blame Dakota? Of course he'd ditch me as soon as Skye showed any interest.

It was getting dark. I could see the orange sun glowing across the water. At some point, I heard a door open. A minute later, my mom peeked her head into the room.

"Jena?" she asked. "Are you sleeping?"

"Sort of," I mumbled.

"Are you almost ready for dinner? Luce and I are heading to the restaurant in a few minutes."

"What about Skye?"

"She's met some kids and she's going with them to the phosphorescent bay."

My stomach clenched even tighter. "What kids?" I asked.

"A boy named Dakota and his mom and brother. Nice people. They're from Rochester. Want me to ask if you can join them?"

"No thanks," I said weakly. "I don't feel so great."

"Oh, honey." My mom came closer to the bed. As she touched my hair, I bit my lower lip to keep from crying. "Do you think you have heatstroke? Want me to get you some Gatorade?"

"No . . . I just want to sleep."

My mom stayed with me for a few minutes and then left the room. A little while later, Skye walked in. She flipped on the bedside light and began gathering things into her bag. I closed my eyes, pretending to be asleep.

"Jena?" Skye asked, standing over me.

I didn't say anything.

"Jena?"

When I still didn't respond, she switched off the light and headed out the door. Once she was gone, I banged my head against the pillow and began sobbing all over again. My throat was so tight I kept gagging and coughing and dry-heaving.

It's all a lie, I said to myself. Romance. *The Bridges of Madison County*. This notion that some guy is going to swoop in and fall madly in love with me and change my life and make everything perfect. It's one big, horrible lie and I bought it. Hook, line, and ten-thousand-pound sinker.

Or I guess I should say it's a lie for a girl like me. For Skye, that's another story. The first time Dakota kissed me, down at the hot tub, I remember thinking, *This is too good to be true*.

But if something feels too good to be true, maybe it's *not* true. Maybe the truth is that Skye deserves him. She'll always be the winner. And I, pathetically, will always be me.

MAY:
DAKOTA'S STORY

one

My day started out like shit and went downhill from there. It was May 19, which would have been Natalie's eighteenth birthday. Knowing Natalie, she would have forced me to take her out to dinner in Rochester. Someplace fancy I couldn't afford, not on my paycheck from Wegmans, especially not since my dad makes me pay my own car insurance. But Natalie's family has money and she was used to being treated like a princess. After dinner, we would have met up with her cheerleading friends. Someone would have produced a cake, someone else would have brought a chick drink like Mike's Hard Lemonade. Then we would have gone back to my place and gotten it on. Natalie had promised me she was going to ask her doctor for the pill this spring. I used to complain that it was over a year and we were still using condoms.

All of this would have happened, of course, if we hadn't been in one of our breakups. Natalie and I were always taking breaks and getting back together. I'd lost track of how many times she screamed at me that it was over, and then hung up the phone or jumped out of my car, slamming the door. We'd ignore each other for a few weeks. Sometimes I'd start hooking up with another girl. Then I'd run into Natalie at a party and she'd be all over me, saying she loved me. I'd apologize for whatever I'd done to piss her off. We'd patch things up and soon we'd be back on track again.

Natalie used to say, "You're an asshole, Dakota. But you're *my* asshole."

I'd laugh, like it was a compliment. But do you really want your girlfriend to think you're an asshole? Especially if it's sort of your fault that she died.

May 19 was a Friday. I set my alarm for six fifty to give me enough time to shower, shave, and put on my suit for the ceremony at school. But I didn't end up needing the clock because I woke at six thirty with an ice pick crushing my temples. I was really hung over. I stayed up last night until one, messing around on the web and drinking too much Jack and Coke. Anything to get my mind off what was going to happen today.

I kicked aside my sheets and trudged down the hall to take a leak. My dad and I are the only people who live here so it's a guys' bathroom all the way. We rarely put the seat down. The mirror is flecked with toothpaste. The tub has a permanent crud ring. We even keep a container of Vaseline in the medicine cabinet.

A few times a year, my dad hires a cleaning lady. But besides her, and besides Natalie, I can't remember the last female who came upstairs. My mom and brother live in Rochester, a half hour from here. That's how we got divided up when my parents divorced three years ago. In the beginning, my mom used to pick me up for her custody weekends. But then I got my license and started driving into Rochester by myself. These days, I tend to skip visits, especially if I have a wrestling meet or a ball game.

I splashed my face with water. My eyes were bloodshot and my face was pale. I looked like hell. Shit, I *felt* like hell. This is pretty much how it'd been since Coach Ritter pulled me into his office two weeks ago and told me about the ceremony.

Today, on what would have been Natalie's birthday, the school was having a ceremony for her, putting up a plaque and everything. I saw the plaque on Wednesday, when the principal called a bunch of us down to the auditorium to review the specifics of the program. The cheerleaders would kick it off. Then the principal explained how Natalie's parents and older brother would come onstage. They'd do a slide show accompanied by Natalie's favorite playlist. After that, I was supposed to go up to the podium, say a few words about Natalie, and lead everyone to the English corridor, where they'd unveil the plaque.

After the principal explained everything, he hoisted the plaque out of a wooden crate and held it up for all of us to see. It was bronze and big, much bigger than I'd imagined. On the left side, it said:

IN MEMORY OF NATALIE AILEEN BIRCH
DEVOTED DAUGHTER
DEVOTED SISTER
DEVOTED FRIEND
BELOVED MEMBER OF THE
BROCKPORT HIGH SCHOOL COMMUNITY

On the other side, beneath a pair of pom-poms, they had a picture of Natalie. It was taken last fall, before she cut her hair. She'd chopped it up to her ears at the end of October. I only remember that because we were in one of our breakups. She was mad because I bailed on some surprise dinner for her brother. But then I ran into her at a Halloween party. I went with a few guys from wrestling and a carload of cute sophomore girls. At some point, I tweaked Natalie's cat ears and whispered, "I liked your hair better long." By the time we got back together, she was growing it out again.

We all sat there in the auditorium, staring at the plaque. The cheerleaders started crying and wrapping their arms around each other. That's what they did for the entire month after the accident. You'd see clumps of them in the hallway, bawling into tissues. As I reread the plaque, I was frozen in my seat. I'm not a crier, but I could feel a lump in my throat. *I used to talk to that girl five times a day,* I kept thinking. *I knew what her tits felt like, how her skin smelled. I had sex with her, for God's sake.*

So now, here I am, two weeks later. The big day. I downed a couple aspirin and stepped into the shower. As I was drying off, I could hear my dad hollering from his bed. Something about my fucking alarm. I must have forgotten to switch it off when I woke up. My dad is a sheriff who works the first platoon, the night shift. He goes to sleep at six and has threatened to kill me if I disturb him while I'm getting ready for school.

I wrapped my towel around my waist and sprinted back to my room, where I pounded the off button on my clock. Then I pulled on some boxers and dug through my closet for my suit. Coach said I should wear one today, out of respect. He just didn't say for whom. Natalie's family? Natalie? Too bad she's six feet under at Lakeview Cemetery.

Natalie used to go crazy when I wore a suit. She said it turned her on. If she'd seen me today, she would have crawled into my lap and started kissing me, unzipping my pants. I can still feel how her fingers wrapped around my dick, her rings clinking together as her hand moved up and down.

I sat on the edge of my bed and reached into my boxers. But then I pulled my hand out and stood up so quickly I nearly blacked out. I may do some asshole things, but I can't jerk off to a dead girl.

two

Twenty minutes later, I was down in the kitchen eating cold pizza and staring at the speech I was supposed to be reading today. I hate public speaking. It's crazy because I can wear a skintight singlet and wrestle a guy in front of a large crowd without getting nervous. But make me recite an oral report and I'm pissing my pants.

Coach told me that an English teacher offered to help me write this speech.

"Screw English teachers," I told Coach. It was only supposed to be three or four minutes. Plus, I hate how everyone acts like you're retarded if you're not in honors classes and French club. "I'm going to Fredonia in the fall. I know how to put some words together."

"Good luck, Shakespeare," Coach said, slapping my back.

It turns out three minutes is a long time. Also, what do you say about a girl you were on the verge of breaking up with when she died? I spent a week typing pathetic attempts, deleting them, and snapping at whoever had the misfortune of talking to me. Finally, I was at work one night, a few days ago. I'd been stocking milk in the dairy section and happened to say a few choice words to the forklift driver, who then went and complained to my boss. When my boss asked me what was up my ass, I told him about the speech for Natalie.

"Use specific examples," he'd advised. "People like that shit. Oh, and lay off the cursing when you're on the job."

Once I'd finished unloading the heavy cream, I'd grabbed an invoice out of a crate and drafted my speech on the back. As soon as I got home, I shoved it in the folder that the principal gave us, with all the information about today's ceremony, and didn't look at it again until today.

I should probably practice it once or twice, I thought as I washed down my pizza with some Coke. *Maybe even time myself.* I glanced at the clock on my phone, and began reading out loud:

"Natalie Birch and I were going out since fall of junior year. She was a great girl and a talented cheerleader. Everyone who met Natalie loved her. She was really funny and she always made people laugh. Also, she wasn't scared to say what was on her mind, especially to guys like me. And she'd kill you if you called her Nat, so don't even try.

"Natalie was always the one to decorate your locker on your birthday and bake you cookies and text you all day. Sometimes she'd get mad at me if I forgot our anniversaries, but then she'd make me buy her something expensive. That was something else about Natalie. She liked shopping and she definitely liked nice things.

"Another thing about Natalie is that she once told me she wanted to be remembered forever. By putting up this plaque today, I guess that's going to happen."

As soon as I was done reading, I checked the time. One measly minute. Fuck.

My cell phone rang. I glanced at the name and then quickly grabbed it before it woke up my dad again.

"What's up, Mom?"

"Hey, Dakota. Are you awake yet?"

"Uh, no. I'm fast asleep."

"But it's seven-oh-five!" she said. "School starts in half an hour."

"I'm joking, Mom. I'm about to leave."

She was quiet, stewing. I couldn't think of anything to say. Yet another bonding moment in our relationship.

"I wanted to remind you to call Pauline," she said after a moment. "It's her birthday."

I forgot that my grandmother and Natalie had the same birthday. When we discovered that at some point, Natalie had acted like it was an earth-shattering coincidence, a sign that things were meant to be. "Meant to be *what*?" I'd asked. My mom's mother is a bitch. No big prize to share a birthday with her.

"You didn't call her on Mother's Day," my mom added. "She's still upset about that."

Typical Pauline. She's never shown interest in me, actively despises my father, and has forbidden my brother and me to call her Grandma. And then she'd be in a huff because I didn't celebrate Mother's Day with her.

"She's not even *my* mom," I said. "Isn't it your job to call her on Mother's Day?"

"*Dakota,*" my mom said. "Please just wish her happy birthday. Please."

"Fine," I said.

"Do you have her number in Knolls Landing?"

I tried to remember the last time I called my grand-parents at their lake house. It's two hours from here, but I hadn't been there since early high school.

My mom began reciting the number. I copied it down on the paper next to my speech.

"Have a nice day at school," she said when she was done. "Do you have anything fun planned?"

I thought about Natalie's ceremony. I'd mentioned it to my dad, but I hadn't told my mom about it. I just assumed she knew, like maybe my dad would have told her. After Natalie died, my dad had called my mom to talk about whether I needed to see a therapist. In the end, my mom decided it made more sense to take my little brother and me to a fancy resort in the Caribbean, to help get my mind off things. The problem is, I can't spend seven consecutive hours around my mom. Forget seven days. My mom and I argued the whole time and my brother completely checked out, as usual, and I hooked up with some girl and then blew her off for her friend, who turned out to be a bitch. All around, the trip was a mighty success.

"Not really, Mom," I said after a long pause. "It's just a regular day."

* * *

After my mom and I hung up, I headed back upstairs. I rubbed some gel in my hair, straightened my tie, and then, at the last minute, poured a few inches of Jack Daniel's in my Blue Devils sports bottle.

On my way back through the kitchen, I scooped up the folder with the ceremony information and the hall pass to get us out of class. There, in the folder, was a photocopy of the news article from the day after the car accident. I don't know why the principal included it in the packet. Maybe to remind us. Like we're going to forget.

I didn't read any articles about the crash when it happened. I knew Natalie was dead. What more did I have to learn? I was one of the first kids to find out because, that night, my dad's patrol car pulled into the driveway. It was around eleven thirty and I was in bed. I heard my dad's shoes clomp up the stairs and pause outside my room. He'd sat on the edge of my mattress and told me how his lieutenant heard it over the air and called him because he knew I went to the same high school. When my dad found out it was Natalie, he drove home to tell me.

Now, standing in the kitchen, I pulled the article out of the packet. It was the cover story in the *Democrat and Chronicle*.

Student Athletes Killed
in Head-on Crash

(February 3) A collision killed two Brock-port High School students as they traveled home from a varsity basketball game yesterday evening. The Ford Focus driven by one of the victims, Jake Kulowski, 17, had just passed a vehicle on Penfield Road when it swerved into oncoming traffic and hit a cement truck, Lieu-tenant Mark Johnson said.

Kulowski was pronounced dead at the scene. The only passenger in the silver Focus, Natalie Birch, 17, was taken by ambulance to Strong Memorial Hospital but died in transport. The truck driver was treated for minor injuries and released late last night.

Kulowski was a junior at Brockport High School and a star soccer player. Birch was a senior, an honors student, and a cheerleader. According to Brockport High School principal Elliot Kerry, Natalie cheered the basketball team to victory at the game in Penfield yes-terday evening. School policy dictates that all players and cheerleaders must ride back to Brockport in buses. But an hour after the game, Natalie was not to be found.

"We waited until ten," Tamara Hedding, the girls' cheerleading coach said. "She wasn't answering her phone. Finally we had to leave."

Details of the events after the game are under investigation.

Brockport High School will remain open for the remainder of the week. Grief counselors will be available for any student or faculty in need.

Goddamn.

I crumpled the article, filled the rest of my sports bottle with Coke, and walked out to my car.

three

There were rumors.

Back in February, in the days following Natalie's death, everyone was whispering about what she was doing in Jake's car. He was a junior and didn't even play basketball. I'd seen him at parties, but had no idea Natalie hung around with him.

Two weeks after the accident, the superintendent summoned me to his office to ask if I knew why Natalie wasn't on the cheerleading bus that night.

"All I know is that she was at the game," I said. "We hadn't talked since that afternoon."

"Anything else, son?"

I shook my head.

The superintendent jotted something on his yellow pad and then said, "I'm sorry about your loss. It's a loss for all of us."

When I left the superintendent's office, I stood in the icy field between the administrative building and the high school. My coat was in my locker, so the wind was whipping onto my neck. I stood there, shivering, wondering if I should go back inside and tell the superintendent about the fight. I hadn't told anyone about it and, honestly, I wasn't planning to. It was wrecking my life enough already. I'd been having stomach pain all week and I even saw blood when I took a shit. It was probably another ulcer, like the one I had after my parents split up.

Finally, I got in my car, cranked the heat, and ditched school for the rest of the day. But I couldn't stop thinking about how Natalie and I had fought on the afternoon of the Penfield game. We were walking to my car, out in the student parking lot. Natalie was wearing her cheering uniform. She had her jacket on, but her short skirt showed off her legs, which were covered in goose bumps.

We were planning to drive to Taco Bell and grab a salad before her game. The bus was leaving for Penfield at four and Natalie was hell-bent on getting me to follow behind in my car and watch her cheer. I hadn't been to any of her games that season and it was pissing her off. Most days I had wrestling, or a bunch of us stayed after to lift in the weight room. But Coach had given us the afternoon off and the janitors were disinfecting the equipment. I was planning to go home and chill out, but Natalie kept bugging me about the game. When I said I wasn't in the mood, she took it as a personal attack.

"I come to your meets," she said as we approached my car. "I even go to those stupid tournaments. Do you think I like wrestling? Do you have any idea how bad it smells in there?"

I clicked the button to unlock the doors. "If you don't like it, don't come."

Natalie planted her hands on her hips. "You should be more interested in what I do. You should be more supportive of me. I'm your *girlfriend*, after all."

"I'm interested," I said even though, at the moment, I was tempted to tell her that cheering is a lame excuse for a sport. I know cheerleaders can jump high and scream loud, but other than checking out their asses when they're lunging into the air, no one really cares about them.

"If you're not interested," Natalie said, "maybe I'll find someone who is."

I climbed into my car. "Be sure to send me a wedding invitation."

"Fuck you," Natalie said. Then she turned and stomped toward the school.

I tore out of the parking lot. When I got home, I watched TV, getting up only to microwave some chicken. Natalie didn't call my cell all evening and I didn't try her either. I figured we were headed toward another breakup and, to be perfectly honest, I was fine with it.

By the time I went to bed, I was actually thinking that maybe this time it'd be for good. Maybe I'd find a younger girl, someone who looked up to me. Natalie was always treating me like an idiot, yelling at me and expecting me to take it.

The next thing I knew my dad was sitting on my bed, telling me she was dead. That she'd died with some other guy. *Jake Kulowski*, my dad said. *Did you know him?*

That whole night, after my dad told me about the accident, I kept thinking that if I'd gone to the Penfield game, Natalie wouldn't have run off with Jake. She would have taken the bus. Or maybe I would have driven her home. The girls' cheerleading coach liked me, so she probably would have let me do it. I never would have attempted to pass on that stretch of Penfield Road. I definitely never would have crashed into a cement truck.

four

As I crossed the lawn into school, I loosened my tie
around my neck. It was a warm spring morning, too
hot for a suit. Too hot for school, actually, for being
cramped up at a desk, acting like I'm paying attention.
I reminded myself that there's only five weeks left until
graduation. Hopefully summer will fly. By the end of
August, I'm off to Fredonia and away from all this.

"Dakota!"

I turned around. Gina Robinson was waving and
calling my name.

"Nice suit," she said as she caught up with me.

"Thanks."

Gina was a cheerleader friend of Natalie's and one
of the girls who was going to speak at the ceremony
today. I always had the feeling Gina wanted to hook

up with me, even back when Natalie was alive. She wasn't my type, though. She had bulging eyes, almost like someone was strangling her. Also, Gina was a notorious gossip. Get together with her and the next day the whole school will be blabbing about the size of your dick.

"How're you feeling about today?" Gina asked as she fell into stride next to me.

I shrugged.

"Have you heard about the poem?" Gina asked.

"What poem?"

"Supposedly Natalie used to write poetry," Gina said. "I didn't know that about her, did you?"

I shook my head.

Gina continued. "I guess Jake's mom found this poem in his stuff that Natalie wrote for him. It was from the week before they died. She gave it to Natalie's family. Supposedly it's really deep. Natalie's brother is going to read it today."

I stared at Gina.

"I know," Gina said, leveling her bug eyes at me. "I thought you'd want to know about that."

I skipped homeroom. I shoved my bag into my locker, grabbed my iPod and the folder with the hall pass, and headed to the locker room. No one was around, so I sat on a long bench and lowered my face in my hands. I could hear the principal reciting the Pledge. I reached for my sports bottle and took a quick taste. Next came the girls' and boys' baseball scores from yesterday's game. We creamed Rush-Henrietta six to nothing. My buddies and I were riding high at Burger King last night, everyone slapping my back because I batted in two runs.

The principal downshifted to his soberest tone. "The ceremony for Natalie Birch will commence in the auditorium at nine o'clock," he said. "Attendance is mandatory. Students, come directly to the auditorium after first period. Anyone participating in the program should report to the auditorium at eight forty-five."

I clutched my gut. I could feel the pain ripping into my stomach. I took another sip of Jack and Coke, changed into shorts, and headed downstairs.

When I stepped into the weight room, I spotted Coach Ritter at his desk. He's been my wrestling coach for the past four years. Even though it's baseball season, he's still Coach to me. Anyone who doesn't do wrestling doesn't get it. It's not like the other sports where you've got a whole team to back you up. With wrestling, it's one-on-one, so there's this instant camaraderie, a brotherhood of wrestlers. Only another wrestler will understand the pain you go through, how much you hate dropping weight, and how, as much as the sport sucks, you keep coming back for more.

Coach used to wrestle in high school and college, so he's more like one of the guys than the other teachers. He teaches chemistry, but he also has a small office in the back of the weight room. Sometimes I go in there and talk with him. He can be tough, but he's the only adult here who doesn't treat me like a dumb jock. He was the person who encouraged me to apply to Fredonia. I was thinking I'd go to MCC, do community college for a year, but he said it'd be good for me to get away from home.

"Hey, Ritter," I called out to him.

Coach looked up from his desk and saluted me.

"Okay if I work out?" I asked.

"Where're you supposed to be?"

I held up the pass from the principal.

"Go for it," Coach said. "But easy on the biceps. I heard you batted in two runs yesterday."

I put on my iPod, pumped some heavy metal, and warmed up on the treadmill. I ran for a few minutes at a steady five mph jog and then turned it up to ten.

As my sneakers pounded against the track, I began to forget Natalie, that poem, the ceremony. Whenever she drifted into my mind, I'd hit the arrow to increase my speed.

By the time I moved on to biceps, I was dripping with sweat. Guys won't admit it, but we're all obsessed with our biceps. I did three sets of ten reps, thirty-five pounds on each side. I knew I was pushing it, especially since we have practice this afternoon, but what the fuck. That was going to be my motto today. What the fuck.

Now I was ready to start benching. I glanced into Coach's office. He was on a call, his chair rotated so he was facing the wall. He'd murder me if he knew I was benching without a spotter, but there was no one else in the weight room. And, besides, you'd have to be an idiot to drop the bar on yourself.

I headed over to the bench press. Back in wrestling season, I was in prime shape. I was wrestling at 145 and benching as much as 150. Now I'm a fat slob, my weight probably up to 158 or 159. And the last time I benched, I couldn't do more than 120. Damn depressing.

I put seventy on both sides. Then, after another glance at Coach's back, I added another five pounds each. One-fifty, baby. Time to get serious.

I lay down on the bench, gripped my hands on the bar, and unracked the weights. *Oh, man,* I thought as I brought it down. I was one weak motherfucker. As I heaved it up, my arms were trembling so bad I thought they might buckle. But I kept—*two*—pumping even though—*three*—the blood was rushing to my—*four*—head and I was struggling to—*five*—

"What the hell are you doing, Evans?"

Breathe.

Coach was standing above me. He wrangled the bar out of my fists and fitted it onto the rack. "I said, what the hell are you doing?"

"I'm benching," I sputtered.

"Without a spotter?" Coach barked. "Are you trying to kill yourself?"

I didn't say anything. Sometimes you just have to wait for Coach to finish. He cools off quickly.

"Listen—" Coach slipped twenty pounds off each side. "You do whatever you want on your time, but you're not going to injure yourself on my watch. I'll spot you, but take it easy. You were only doing one-twenty last week."

Coach had me on 110 now. My pecs were killing and my triceps were strained, but I wasn't about to tell him

I couldn't do any more.

I got my hands back in position. Coach unracked the bar again. I pumped out ten and then stared up at the ceiling, panting. I was just lifting my arms to do a final set when Coach said, "Hey, Evans, it's almost eight thirty. You have to be up at the auditorium in fifteen minutes."

I didn't say anything as I gripped the bar. Coach unracked it and I did ten more reps, slower this time. When I was done, I sank my arms onto my chest. Baseball practice was going to be hell this afternoon.

Coach glanced at his watch and then gave me a long look. "You okay about today?"

"Yeah." I wiped the sweat from my forehead and got up off the bench. "I'll be fine."

No one was in the locker room. I stripped down, grabbed a towel from the spare locker in the back, and headed to the showers. I cranked the water and stood under the spray, hoping the heat would ease the pain. I totally overdid it just now. Too much weight, not enough warm-up. I've been doing sports my whole life. I should have known better.

As I was drying off, I couldn't stop thinking about what Gina said. I can't believe Natalie wrote a poem for Jake. So that means there was definitely something going on between them when they died. I guess I'm not surprised. Natalie and I were on thin ice anyway. I just don't understand why she didn't end it with me before she began composing love sonnets for him.

It was five to nine as I crossed the atrium and headed toward the auditorium. There were kids pouring in from everywhere, chatting as they filed through the double doors. Whenever someone spotted me, they stared. That's how it was after Natalie died, that expression of pity and intrigue and even a little respect.

I wondered how they'd look at me after Natalie's brother read the poem. Then I'd have to walk up on the stage and, like an idiot, recite my speech about how I was her boyfriend and she was so great.

My stomach began burning. I veered into the bathroom and hunched over the sink. I splashed my face with water and then headed outside again. Just as I was rounding the corner, I practically slammed into Natalie's brother.

"What's up?" I said, stepping back. I hadn't seen Timon Birch since the funeral in February. He was a junior at Dartmouth and a complete prick. It helped that he was away at college the whole time Natalie and I were together. But whenever he came home, I always got this condescending vibe from him, like he thought I was some low-class cop's kid. I had the last laugh, though, because when he was backpacking in Europe last summer, Natalie went down on me in his brand-new Prius.

Timon was tall, practically a head above me, with an annoying flop of Ivy League hair. He smirked at me, but didn't say anything.

I tensed my jaw. "I said *what's up?*"

Timon muttered something that sounded like *Hmph*.

I was not in the mood for this. "Have you got a problem?"

"I'm just surprised to see you here," Timon said.

"What's that supposed to mean?" I asked.

"It's not like you're going to be reflected in the most positive light."

"Are you talking about that poem?"

"You want to hear it?" Timon reached into his pants pocket.

I could feel anger radiating through my body. "Are you trying to fuck with me?"

Timon unfolded the paper in his hands. As soon as I saw it, my stomach lurched. That was Natalie's stationery, for sure. The same stuff she used when she slipped notes in my locker. I hadn't thought about that since she died, how they always smelled like vanilla and fresh ink.

"For Jake." Timon glanced down at me. *"And so, finally, it makes sense. Even on a February night, I can feel flowers, sing songs, soak in sun—"*

"Shut the fuck up, okay?" I shouted, pushing him in the shoulder.

A hush fell over the atrium. Kids hurried back from the doors that lead into the auditorium and gathered around us.

"What the hell are you trying to prove?" I asked. "That your sister was cheating on me? Great. Thanks."

"I'm just saying"—Timon rubbed his shoulder— "that you thought you could treat her like crap and she'd take it. But she didn't put up with all your shit. She had her own things going on."

I visualized slamming his head into the wall, felt the satisfying crack of his skull.

Timon continued. "You know that necklace Natalie got you in the Bahamas?"

"What about it?" I asked, clenching my fists. Natalie and I had only been together a few months when she went on a vacation with her family. Things were good with us back then. We hadn't even broken up once. We chatted online every day of her trip and, when she got home, she brought me a T-shirt and a white puka-shell necklace. The shirt got wrecked in the dryer, but I still wear the necklace every day.

"Some guy at our resort gave it to her," Timon said, "to remember the time they spent together. You know, the long walks on the beach, the—"

I shoved Timon in the chest. He went stumbling backward a few steps but then regained his footing, lunged forward, and pushed me hard. I pushed him again. He drew his arm to punch me, but before he could make contact I dropped onto my knee, wrapped my arms around his legs, and drove my shoulder into him.

Timon fell to the ground with me straddling him. I was just getting ready to pound his face when, all of a sudden, I felt intense pain. Someone was gripping my shoulder, yanking me off Timon, shoving me into the wall.

"WHAT THE HELL ARE YOU DOING?" Coach Ritter shouted. He was breathing fast and I could see veins pulsing in his temples.

I craned my head around Coach. Timon was standing up, shaking out his suit. A couple girls were fluttering around him, offering to fetch ice from the nurse.

"Come with me," Coach barked, grabbing my elbow.

Neither of us said a word as he steered me through the halls, down the stairs, and into the weight room. He propelled me into his office and jabbed a finger at his chair.

"I'll be back," he said as I slumped down. "Don't move an inch."

five

I got a week's vacation. That's the automatic sentence for fighting. I'd never been suspended before because, other than minor shoving, I hadn't been in full-fledged combat on school premises.

Coach was the one who handed down my punishment. It's usually the vice principal, but I have a feeling he let Ritter do it because of the circumstances, Natalie's ceremony and all. I ended up waiting in Coach's office for an hour, spinning around in his chair, reading the memos on his walls. He was probably up in the auditorium. I wondered what would happen in the slot when I was supposed to give my speech. My name was in the program and everything. I wondered who would lead people down the hall to see Natalie's plaque.

At ten, Coach opened his office door, gestured to the folding chair, and said, "Move it."

I stood up, wincing in pain. My left knee was smashed from where I'd dropped onto the floor when I took Timon down.

Coach sat in his chair, leaned forward so he was looking me in the eye, and said, "What the hell were you doing up there, Dakota?"

Coach never calls me by my name. I was in deep shit. I looked down at my shoes. I wasn't going to whine about the crap Timon said to me, how he was asking for it.

"I know emotions were running high," he added, "but I always tell you guys that you've got to walk away. Especially now that you're eighteen. You're not a minor anymore. You don't want people pressing assault charges, do you?"

"No," I said.

"I spoke with Mr. B," Coach said. "You've got five days. Nothing I could do about that."

"What about baseball?"

"Out for a month. That means you'll miss the rest of the year unless you guys win sectionals."

"Shit," I muttered.

"Watch the language," he said, reaching for his

phone. "What's your number?"

"You mean my home number? Who're you call-ing?"

"Parents have to be notified when there's a fight. Mr. B wanted me to get your dad in for a conference, but I convinced him that a phone call would do. It's your first time."

Now this was *really* starting to suck. After fourteen years as a sergeant, my dad had no tolerance for juvenile delinquents. Also, it was just a few minutes after ten, so he was still asleep.

"Your number, Dakota."

I recited the digits. As he dialed, I prayed it would go through to voicemail. I prayed Coach would tone down the description of the fight. I prayed my dad would take Natalie's death into consideration.

"Hi, Mr. Evans? This is Curt Ritter, the wrestling coach over at the high school."

Coach covered the receiver for a second and mouthed, *Wait for me out there*. Then he pointed to the bench press. As I limped outside, he closed the door.

After a few minutes, he emerged from his office. His broad face was stern. "Your dad wants you home right now," he said.

I stood up slowly. This was going to be fun. People

sometimes say I have a temper, but believe me, it's nothing compared to my dad.

Coach escorted me out of the weight room. When we reached the door, he said, "I expected more from you, Dakota."

I tossed my coat onto the passenger seat and pulled out of the student parking lot. It was ten twenty on Friday morning. It's not like I love school, but no one wants to get suspended. And now baseball season was fucked. The guys were going to kill me. I'm always good for a run or two. Maybe three if I'm pumped.

It was all that prick Timon's fault. Timon and his parents. What were they thinking, picking a poem that Natalie wrote for Jake? Did they hate me that much? They weren't exactly warm and fuzzy to me at the funeral, but her dad did shake my hand and her mom gave me a weepy hug. Plus, they can't deny that I took Natalie to junior prom and two Winter Balls, and they even brought me up to their camp in the Adirondacks last summer. If she was so into poetry, I'm sure they could have unearthed a few words she'd put together about me. She was always carrying around that journal.

Then again, Natalie used to joke that she only wrote

in her journal when she was mad at me. Her family probably read it after she died. They probably think I'm an asshole. Maybe I *was* an asshole at times, but Timon didn't have to rub my face in it, telling me how Natalie got my necklace from some guy she had a fling with in the Bahamas.

I should drive over to the Birches' house and find Timon, finish what he started. He's tall, but he didn't seem that tough. Except, knowing Timon, he probably *would* press assault changes.

When I hit Allen Street, I turned left. But instead of going the direct route to my house, I cut onto Holley, which runs into Redman Road. That's the long way. I'm not such an idiot that I'd race home just to get the shit kicked out of me.

I ended up climbing the locks. They're over by the canal, near the college parking lot on the way to Redman Road. It's a tall steel tower on the south bank of the Erie Canal, about thirty feet above the water. There's a ladder running up one side. A few times, on warm nights, some of my buddies and I have climbed up here to drink. I've heard about SUNY students getting wasted on the locks and jumping into the canal. Judging by the color of the water, you'd have to be pretty gone to do that.

My biceps were strained and my knee was bruised, so it killed to grasp the rungs. But once I was at the top I could feel the stress easing up. I was planning to hang out here for a few minutes, get a small buzz going, enough to help me face my dad.

The sky was clear blue, just a few clouds up north near Lake Ontario. I could see a guy jogging along the towpath, a bottle of water in his hand. A woman was walking her dachshund on the other side. His snout was low to the ground, following some scent.

I took a sip from my sports bottle and peered over the edge. Man, it was a long fucking way down. I'm surprised that those guys who dive from here actually live to tell. If I jumped off, it'd be instant suicide, especially if I hit one of those rocks lining the side of the canal.

I scooted back from the edge. I may do some crazy things, but I'm not the suicide type. The whole concept of suicide freaks the shit out of me, deciding one day, *Hey, I'm going to end my life*. Scary as hell. Especially now that I know what it's like when someone actually dies.

When I was at that resort my mom took me to after Natalie died, the girl I hooked up with, Jena, found a suicide note on the edge of the hot tub. It was all about how some person wants to slice their wrists and bleed on a bed. When I read it, I thought I was going to vomit. I kept picturing an ambulance removing a corpse from the hotel, which then made me think about Natalie, wonder if she'd been in a body bag.

Jena was cute, the smart, cheerful type. The only problem was, I got the feeling she liked me too much, thought I was going to be her Prince Charming. Also, she was there with a gorgeous friend who I happened to be alone with on the beach one afternoon. We played a few rounds of gin rummy and at first she was flirtatious, even coming with me on a boat ride that night. But as soon as I tried to touch her she went ice cold, barely talking to me. She split so quickly she left her cards in our rental car, but I could never track her down to give them back.

Maybe it wasn't the nicest thing in the world to blow off one girl for her hotter friend, but it's not as if Jena and I had an official commitment. Not like Natalie and me, which makes it all the more messed up to find out she cheated on me even in the beginning, with a guy in the Bahamas.

That fucking necklace.

I unscrewed it from my neck and chucked it toward

the canal. It landed with a plunk and disappeared beneath the sludgy water.

People would probably be shocked to discover this, but I never actually cheated on Natalie. Sure, I flirted with girls. But I never even kissed anyone else. Of course, when Natalie and I were in one of our break-ups, I did whatever I wanted. It was amazing how quickly the sophomore girls would put out, almost like they had something to prove.

Whenever we made up, Natalie would be pissed. "How could you have been with that slut, Dakota?" she'd say. "Did you look at her nose? She's not even cute!"

I knew better than to defend myself, so I'd reassure Natalie that I was drunk when it happened, that she was much sexier than any of them.

"Hey, buddy, what's going on up there?"

I glanced over the edge of the lock.

Fuck.

A patrol car was parked next to mine and I could see two cops. A chunky one was hanging out near the cars, his hand positioned on his right hip. The other, a tall guy, was hiking up the incline toward the canal. I quickly stuffed my sports bottle under the metal grate.

At least it was the Brockport Police. Better than the sheriff's office because then it'd get back to my dad.

"Everything okay up there?" the tall cop asked, peering up at me.

"Yes, sir," I called down to him. I know from my dad that it's key to cooperate with police. Most of them start off calm, but if you get mouthy they're going to escalate things. Next thing you know you're at the station getting fingerprinted.

"Are you coming down or do you need me to get you?"

"No, sir," I said. "Sorry. I'm coming down."

I swallowed hard, hoping he wouldn't smell the Jack on my breath, and lowered my foot onto the top rung. My knee was killing and my pecs felt like they were going to tear and the alcohol was screwing with my coordination. But I could feel this guy watching me closely, so I directed all my concentration on climbing, climbing, climbing—

My foot missed a rung and I slipped. I quickly caught myself, but my heart was racing so fast I could barely hold on.

"You okay?"

"Yeah," I said. I took a deep breath and resumed my descent.

When I reached the bottom, I brushed my hair out of my face. Sweat was pouring down my forehead. So much for calm and collected.

The cop stepped closer to me and shielded his eyes with his hand. "So what was going on up there?"

"Nothing much," I said. "Just hanging out."

"We got a call from the dispatcher." He gestured to the top of the lock. "That's considered trespassing."

"Sorry," I said, grinding the grass with my foot. "I didn't know that."

"How old are you?"

"Eighteen."

"Are you supposed to be in school?" he asked.

"I got suspended today."

"Bad day, huh?"

"You could say that." I kicked at some more grass and stumbled a little.

The officer stared hard at me. "Have you been drinking?"

I shrugged.

"Where's the alcohol?"

I didn't say anything. It wasn't like I could deny it, especially if he climbed the lock and found my sports bottle, but I wasn't going to admit anything, either.

"What's your name?" he asked.

"Dakota Evans."

"Well, Dakota," he said, "you seem like a nice kid, so I'm not going to run a Breathalyzer. But you should know that possession of alcohol is illegal for anyone under twenty-one. Also, the village of Brockport has an ordinance against open containers." He turned and gestured toward the parking lot. "That your car?"

"Yeah," I said quietly.

"One violation against the open-container ordinance and we can suspend your license. And you don't even have to be driving for that. But, as I said, you seem like a nice kid. Do you have any prior record?"

I shook my head.

The officer glanced toward the other cop and then said, "I'm just going to give you a warning. Between you and me. Quit it with the drinking and the trespassing and you'll be okay."

I was about to drop to the ground and kiss his feet when he cleared his throat. "So what's your parents' number?"

My stomach lurched. "My parents?"

"I can't send you in a car like this."

"Can I call a friend? Or can't I just walk home? I live over on Meadowview Drive."

"Hey, buddy." The officer straightened up. "You'd

rather get an appearance ticket?"

I wondered whether I should give him my mom's number. No, she wouldn't know how to deal with this. Besides, she'd just refer him to my dad.

And so, for the second time that morning, I recited my dad's number. The officer jotted it down on his pad. As I stood there dying a brutal death, he pulled out his phone and began dialing.

six

Five minutes later, my dad pulled up. He parked, got out, and strode over to where I was standing next to the officers.

"Wait in my car," he hissed without even looking at me.

Then he smiled at the men and shook their hands. As I was walking away, I heard him mention something about C-zone, and the chunky officer said a guy's name and they both laughed.

After a few minutes, the officers got in their patrol car and my dad headed toward me. As he opened the door, he held up his hand as if to say: *Not a goddamn word.* Then he shifted into gear and we drove in silence across the parking lot and down Holley Street. When we pulled into our driveway, he turned to me and said,

"Give me your keys."

I reached in my pocket and tossed him my keys. He pried my car key off the ring and handed the rest back to me. Then he stepped out of the car, walked down the driveway, and took a right on Meadowview. I watched him for a minute and then got out of the car and hobbled into the house.

When my dad returned with my car, I was sitting at the kitchen table, sipping some water.

"Dad?"

He held up his hand again. His face was flushed, angry. "Your mother is going to call you."

"Mom? Why?"

He walked past me, stomped up the stairs, and slammed his door.

The phone rang a few minutes later. I was laying on my bed. I considered letting my mom go through to voicemail, but she'd just call my dad and the last thing I wanted was for him to storm into my room and chew me out for not answering.

"Hey, Mom," I said, lifting the phone to my ear.

"You got in some trouble this morning," she said.

Leave it to Melinda Evans to state the obvious.

"Your father and I talked," she said. "It sounds like things are getting out of control for you. We both decided you need a change of scenery."

Oh, Jesus, I thought, wondering where this was headed.

"You're going to stay with your grandparents for the week that you're suspended. No protests."

I held my breath, hoping she'd say my Idaho grandparents. They're clueless, but okay. Unlike my mom's parents, who are downright assholes.

"I'll drive you to Knolls Landing at nine tomorrow," my mom added.

There were a million things running through my head, like how could they send me to Pauline and Bill's, who don't like me, who barely like *her*?

"Can't I just drive myself?" I asked.

"Your father didn't tell you?"

"Tell me what?"

"He's taking away your car," my mom said.

I inhaled sharply. After all the shitty things that had happened today, I hadn't realized it could get worse.

"See you tomorrow," she added. "Be ready."

seven

When my mom pulled into the driveway the next morning, she honked twice. My dad was still sleeping. He didn't work last night, but he keeps the same hours seven days a week. I grabbed my bag, checked to make sure I'd remembered my iPod, and then headed outside. My mom was in the driver's seat, her blazer neatly pressed, her brown hair pulled in a low ponytail.

She popped the trunk. I threw in my stuff. As I was buckling my seat belt, she pointed her manicured finger in my direction and said, "I am *not* happy with you right now."

"It's great to see you, too," I said as she reversed onto Meadowview Drive.

I wasn't exactly in the best mood. The guys on the team kept texting last night, giving me hell for fucking up baseball season. And then, when I called Wegmans to tell my manager I'd be away for the week, he said he couldn't guarantee my shifts when I returned.

For the first half hour of the drive, my mom didn't say a word to me. Her phone kept ringing. By the third call, she clipped on her earpiece and answered it. It sounded like some woman she exercises with because my mom apologized for missing her at the gym. "A small problem came up," my mom said. "I'll be there next Saturday."

So that's what I was to her. A small problem.

After she hung up, my mom hit a button on her phone. "Hey, Owen," she said. "I just wanted to make sure you found that cinnamon roll I left on the counter."

She checks to see if my brother eats breakfast? He's fifteen, for God's sake.

My mom proceeded to tell Owen there was grape-fruit juice in the fridge and cash on the table. I was just wondering whether she was going to instruct him to shake his dick after he pissed when she said, "And don't stay in front of that computer all day. It's a beautiful spring morning. Take a bike ride or something."

She tells him to take a bike ride?

As soon as my mom hung up, I said, "You need to let

up on Owen. You baby him too much. You need to let him take care of himself more, become a man."

"Thanks," my mom said, "but I'll pass on your parenting advice."

"As long as you're okay having a wuss for a son."

"Leave Owen alone," my mom snapped, turning on the radio. "He's doing fine."

Leave Owen alone. That was a phrase I'd heard my entire life. Owen was only two and a half years younger than me, but my mom was so protective of him you'd think he was an infant. He'd always been on the scrawny side, not particularly athletic. My dad used to get mad at him for never wanting to play ball with us. That was back when we all lived together. Sometimes, when Owen and I argued, I'd knock him around a little. But as soon as my mom showed up she'd scramble to my brother's defense, grounding me without even hearing both sides of the story.

A few minutes later, as we were cruising along the thruway, my mom turned to me. "Do you want to tell me what happened yesterday?"

"Would it help?" I asked.

"Help what?"

"It sounds like you've already cast your judgment."

"Tackling Natalie's brother, Dakota? Getting suspended? Drinking and trespassing? Do I have much of a choice?"

"That's what I'm saying," I muttered.

My mom cracked a Diet Pepsi. I put on my iPod and stared out the window. After a while, we exited the thruway. We passed gas stations and cornfields and rusty trailer homes. Finally, I could see the tip of Cayuga Lake. It's forty miles long and narrow, like a river. My grandparents spend every summer in their cabin halfway up the lake, but we rarely visit them here. Usually my mom brings Owen and me to their Florida condo in the winter, or they come into Rochester and meet us for brunch in the summer.

As we turned onto the dirt road that leads to their house, my mom gestured for me to remove my iPod. I popped out one ear.

"You didn't call Pauline for her birthday yesterday," my mom said. "She wasn't happy about that."

"I had other things on my mind," I said.

"The world doesn't revolve around you, Dakota."

"Is that *your* parental advice for the day?"

"You know what?" my mom said. "Screw you."

"Your mothering techniques are getting better and better," I said.

Neither of us spoke for the rest of the drive.

* * *

It took Pauline thirty seconds to insult my mom. We'd just walked into the main room of the cabin. I was carrying my bag. My mom had a stack of presents for her mother. Bill was at the counter, slicing peaches. Pauline was at the dining-room table, thumbing through the newspaper. She looked up, brushed back a wisp of silver hair, and said, "You've gotten fat, Melinda."

"I'm the same as always," my mom protested.

"So you're saying you've always been fat?" Pauline looked back down at the newspaper. "I don't think so."

"Well, happy birthday, Mom." My mom set the gifts on a chair. "Hi, Dad."

Bill pecked my mom on the cheek. As he was shaking my hand, Pauline glanced up again. "Hi, Dakota," she said to me. And then, to my mom, she added, "So he's gotten himself into trouble?"

"Can we talk about this privately?" my mom asked.

"Bill," Pauline said to my grandfather, "bring him upstairs. And remind him to take off those sneakers."

I kicked my sneakers onto the doormat. It was weird the way she was talking about me like I wasn't here. As Bill shuffled up the stairs, I tried to catch his eye, have a male-bonding moment at the sake of the ladies. But no luck. Bill had this flat expression on his face as he stared past me. I think he's still in his sixties, but he's bald and his shoulders are stooped, probably from a lifetime of being henpecked by Pauline.

We entered the small bedroom at the end of the hall. It's the same room Owen and I stayed in when we came here three or four years ago. Bill handed me a towel, showed me how to work the thermostat, and quickly left. I tossed my bag in a corner, dropped onto the bed, and pumped up my iPod.

A few minutes later, my mom came upstairs.

"You okay?" she asked, hovering in the doorway.

I took my music out of one ear. "What do you think?"

My mom sighed. "I'll see you next Saturday."

"You're seriously leaving me here?"

"I'll call you."

"Don't trouble yourself," I said, shoving my earphone back in.

My mom closed the door and went to her car.

At dinner that night, Pauline stabbed a leaf of lettuce. "You're looking more and more like your father," she said, angling her fork into her mouth.

That's all we were eating, by the way. Lettuce with steamed broccoli and tofu. No wonder Bill was such a wuss. I should take him out for a burger while I'm here.

"I hear you're going to Fredonia," Pauline said after a minute.

"Yeah," I said.

"Good school," Bill said.

"But not the best," Pauline added.

"Of course not. If you're going for the best state," Bill said, "it's got to be Cornell's ag school."

After dinner, Bill served us leftover birthday cake. As Pauline licked her final dab of frosting, she said, "You didn't call me yesterday."

"I had other things going on," I said. And then, for some reason, I added, "It was my girlfriend's birthday."

Pauline set down her fork. "You have a new girlfriend already? I thought your girlfriend died."

"No," I said quietly. "It was the dead one's birthday."

Pauline and Bill looked at each other and then, without another word, cleared their plates, piled them into the sink, and retreated to the TV room.

eight

Talk about exile. Knolls Landing was so far off the grid I didn't even get cell phone reception. Not that I wanted to spill my soul to anyone, but it might have been nice to text a few guys, see if we won against Spencerport. I had my computer with me, but I couldn't look up the game because they didn't have Internet access here. Fucking Dark Ages.

I actually *needed* to get online because I was supposed to email my homework assignments to a few teachers who don't understand that the sole perk of suspension is the break from school. I barely cared about grades at this point, but the last thing I wanted was for an F to wreck my chances of going to Fredonia. I told my grandparents about the homework and suggested maybe I could borrow their car and drive into town, find someplace that has wireless.

"No way," Pauline said. "Not after the trouble you got into back home."

That's when Bill dug this ancient fax machine out of a downstairs closet. "Fax it in," he said in his typical monotone.

"Do you have a printer here?" I asked.

Bill shook his head.

"But I'd have to print out my homework to fax it in," I said.

"Guess you'll be handwriting your assignments," Pauline said, clucking her tongue.

I made a face.

"Your generation," Pauline said as she retrieved two yellow slickers from the hall closet, "is way too dependent on technology. It's frightening, really."

I wanted to tell her that *she* was the frightening one here, but before I could respond she was already out the door.

This was Wednesday. It had been raining since Saturday night. A cold, driving rain with no end in sight. At first, it hadn't mattered that the weather was shitty because my knee was still wrecked from the fight with Timon and my biceps were still pulled from lifting too much. After a few days, though, I felt much better. But the rain was coming down so hard I could barely step outside without getting soaked.

My grandparents, however, couldn't be stopped. Every morning at nine fifteen, Pauline and Bill donned identical raincoats, boots, and waterproof hats and embarked on a power walk. Their whole joined-at-the-hip thing was freaky. They spooned up their bran cereal together, read the newspaper, went on their walk, ate their lunch, took their nap, watched their shows—and never once invited me to join them. The only thing we all did was dinner, and even then they mainly talked to each other. It's not like I'm the guest of honor at my dad's house, but it was strange to feel so unwelcome. My mom was their only child, growing up in nearby Syracuse. I had to wonder if she felt this way too.

The days were long in Knolls Landing. I watched whatever I could find on their four staticky channels. I wrote out my homework until my fingers were indented, and then faxed it into school. For the rest of the time, I lay on the bed listening to music. That's when my stomach burned the worst.

Mostly, as I lay there, I wondered about Natalie and Jake, about that poem Timon had begun reciting when I slugged him. I could only remember one part, something about "feeling the flowers," whatever *that* means. Part of me wanted to know the rest. I wanted to know what Natalie could say to Jake that she couldn't say to me. I knew it would fuck me up even more, but not knowing was worse.

If I had wireless, I could find it in a second. Natalie's friends have this tribute blog for her, all these pictures and even some videos of her at cheering competitions. Gina Robinson told me they were going to post coverage of the ceremony. I'm sure they've added . . . what did Timon call the poem? "For Jake." I'm sure they've added "For Jake" by now.

So now the whole world can read Natalie's poem and see how she was in love with Jake Kulowski while she was going out with me. Everyone's probably laughing their asses off at me right now. And here I am, unable to defend myself, banished to the rainy fucking Dark Ages from hell.

On Wednesday night, as Bill did the dishes, Pauline pulled out an old photo album. I was sitting across from her at the dining-room table, spearing the last of my green beans and bemoaning to myself how this is worse than weight-dropping during wrestling season. For a second, as I looked at the leather-bound album,

I thought, *Oh, wow, a grandmother moment.*

"Here he is," Pauline pronounced as she landed on the last page of the album.

"Who?" All I could see were a bunch of upside-down faces.

"The man your mom should have married."

I looked over at Bill but he was turned toward the sink.

"Henry Ruderman." Pauline rotated the album around so I could see the photos. "Melinda went out with him for two years at Colgate. We really thought he was the one."

I glanced at the pictures. Nothing special. Just a younger version of my mom posing next to some guy with fluffy blond hair.

"He became a corporate lawyer in Albany," Pauline added.

By that, she basically meant: *Not a cop like your dad.*

"You know," Pauline said, "the whole thing with your father was a mistake from start to finish."

"Except some mistakes," Bill said as he turned off the faucet, "you simply can't reverse."

"Exactly," Pauline said, closing the album.

I stared at both of them. Natalie used to tell me I

was an asshole. I probably *was* sometimes, but maybe I couldn't help it. My parents have asshole tendencies. My grandparents are *definite* assholes. Maybe there was just no escaping my genes.

Late Wednesday night, the rain finally stopped. On Thursday morning, Pauline and Bill took a power walk and then loaded canvas bags into their trunk. Thursday, they informed me, they drive into town. First a trip to the library, then the co-op for vitamins, then the grocery store.

After they left, I settled at the kitchen table. I had to finish an assignment for politics in government. My handwriting sucks, so I kept making mistakes, crumpling up the paper, and starting again. Finally, I rammed my fist against the table and went in search of Wite-Out.

I was rifling through a desk drawer when the phone rang. I glanced down. No caller ID here in the Dark Ages. I hesitated for a second before picking up.

"Hello?"

"Dakota?" my brother's voice asked.

"*Owen?* Why are you calling here?"

"I have a free period at school. I just wanted to see how you're doing. I tried your cell and it's off."

"You called to see how I'm doing?" I asked. Owen and I never talk on the phone. And in person, it's nothing more than pass the ketchup, where's the remote, it's my turn to take a shower. He isn't the most social person in the world. And I'm not exactly gunning for one of those tight, brotherly friendships.

"I just thought it might be sucking there," Owen said.

"It's definitely sucking."

"They shouldn't have sent you to Pauline and Bill's. You got suspended and climbed the locks. It's not like you murdered anyone."

"Yeah," I said, feeling shittier by the second. "I can't believe my life has come to this."

"That reminds me of this quote I recently heard. Hold on . . . let me look . . ." Owen paused and I could hear him clicking at his laptop. "Here it is. 'Whether or not it is clear to you, no doubt the universe is unfolding as it should.' By some guy named Max Ehrmann. I think it's supposed to mean that even though things suck right now, it's all going to be okay in the end."

"You sound like a chick when you recite quotes," I said. I couldn't help it. I was in a lousy mood and my brother stepped smack into the middle of it. Also, he was being too pushy with the life advice, like he was suddenly going wise on me.

"I sort of liked it," Owen said. "I heard it from a friend."

"A real friend or someone online?"

"I was just trying to be nice."

"Don't."

Neither of us said anything. After a moment, Owen said, "I've got a class in a few minutes. I better go."

"Me too."

We quickly said good-bye and both hung up.

nine

That afternoon, I ran hard. I went down the stairs that lead to the lake, all the way to the end of the gravel road, up the steep hill, back down the hill. Once I reached the lake again, I picked up my speed and began sprinting. The lower road was lined with cabins, but there were only a few cars parked out front. Most of the houses were boarded up. As I ran, I looked out at the lake. It was muddy near the shoreline, but farther out it was blue and sparkling. On the other side of the road were woods and ravines. I remembered hiking in those woods when I was younger. My dad would bring me out there when my grandparents were driving him crazy.

It felt good to be running again, to have my heart pumping. I was just nearing the end of the road when this barefoot little kid, maybe two or three years old, came cruising around the side of a cabin, stumbled in the yard, and fell down.

I stopped quickly. "Are you okay?"

The kid stared at me with huge brown eyes. At first I couldn't tell whether it was a boy or a girl, but then, as it wobbled up again, I noticed nail polish on her toenails, every color of the rainbow.

I pulled my iPod out of my ears. "Are you okay?"

She kept staring at me, but didn't say a word. She had wild black hair, a combination of braids and dreads, and she was wearing an oversized T-shirt.

"Are your parents around?" I asked.

All of a sudden, I heard a voice shouting, "Dewey! Dewey!"

A second later, a light-skinned black woman emerged from the side of the house, spotted us, and said, "There you are, Dew. It looks like you've found a friend."

Then she glanced over at me. "Sorry," she said. "He was chasing a butterfly and he took off on me."

"He?" I asked, gesturing toward his toenails.

"Yeah, I know," she said, smiling. "It's just the two of us out here. We like to have fun."

She was probably in her mid-twenties, wearing jeans and a white undershirt with no bra underneath. I could see the outline of her nipples, full and dark.

"I haven't seen you around before," she said as she scooped up the kid and positioned him on her hip.

"I'm just here for a week," I said. "I'm staying on the upper road."

"I've been renting this place all winter. You're probably the first person under sixty I've seen on the road since January. I'm Shasta, by the way."

"I'm Dakota."

"Cool name," she said.

"You too."

Shasta grinned at me. "Thanks for watching out for Dewey."

"Oh, sure," I said. "He's cute."

"Just like his mama, right?" she said, nuzzling his forehead.

I fitted my earphones back in.

"Have a nice run," she said.

"Thanks," I said. "See you."

"Yeah, see you."

I waved good-bye and kept on running. As I neared the bend in the road, I turned to see if I could catch another glimpse, but they were out of sight.

The next afternoon, I ran by Shasta's cabin again. She wasn't there as I passed. But when I circled back, I spotted her sitting at a table on the deck.

"Hey, Dakota!" She stood up and headed toward me. But then, all of a sudden, she tripped and went flying forward. I started up the stairs, but before I could catch her, she grabbed onto the railing.

"Damn," she said, steadying herself.

"Are you okay?"

"It's this stupid board." She kicked her sandal at a two-by-four protruding from the rest of the deck. "I've asked the owners to fix it and they never seem to get out here. I've tried nailing it myself but it won't stay down."

"It's probably rotten," I said, wiping the sweat off my forehead with my hand.

"Probably." Shasta pulled her braids into a ponytail. "Want to come up for a while, have something to drink?"

"Where's . . ." I paused. I couldn't remember her kid's name.

"Dewey's napping. He went down an hour ago."

I wrapped my earphones around my iPod and followed her across the deck, past a toy truck and a faded plastic rocking horse. She gestured at the table where she'd been sitting. It had an empty coffee cup, a stack of books, and an ashtray with a scattering of cigarette butts.

"What do you want to drink?" Shasta asked as I settled into a chair. "Soda? Beer?"

"You have beer?"

"How old are you?"

"Nineteen," I lied. I hadn't shaved since Monday, but
even so, I doubted I could pass for twenty-one.

"You won't tell anyone?"

I glanced down the empty road. "Who's there to
tell?"

"Hang on." Shasta grabbed her mug and slid open
the glass door.

When she returned, she handed me a Budweiser.
Then she sat next to me, set some black coffee in front
of her, and moved the ashtray over to the railing.

"I don't usually smoke," she said. "I never do it in
front of Dewey."

"Don't worry about it."

Shasta sighed. "It was a long night."

I checked out her face. She was pretty, but her mouth
was drawn and she had circles under her eyes.

"I had one of those conversations with Dewey's
dad," Shasta said after a moment. "We were on the
phone for three hours."

I cracked the beer. "You're not together anymore?"

"Not for two years."

"How old is Dewey?"

"He'll be two in July."

"Oh."

"Exactly." Shasta reached into her pocket for her cigarette pack. "Do you mind?"

"Nah."

She moved the ashtray back to the table and held the cigarette between her lips. As she raised the lighter, she said, "So what are you doing here this week?"

"It's sort of . . . it's complicated."

"Isn't everything?" Shasta said, laughing.

Shasta smoked her cigarette and I drank my beer and we talked about running and the rain and how the lake is still too cold for swimming. But then Shasta sipped some coffee and said, "You know, it pisses me off. A mother would never leave her child. But a dad feels like he can walk away and never look back. Know what I mean?"

I nodded, but I was actually thinking the opposite about me. When my parents divorced, my mom said she could only handle one of us. She picked Owen to move into Rochester with her, which meant I wound up with my dad.

"Don't get me wrong," Shasta said. "Mostly I'm fine out here. But sometimes it's things like that stupid board." Shasta swallowed hard. "Whatever. Don't let me get too deep or anything."

"No," I said. "It's fine."

"Sometimes it just helps to bitch about it."

"Yeah, I know," I said, even though that's definitely not my style, to spill for the sake of spilling.

"Where do you go to school?" Shasta asked.

"Brockport," I said vaguely. There's a SUNY in town, after all. I didn't have to mention I was at the high school. "What about you? Are you in school?"

"Cornell," Shasta said. "I'm getting my PhD in statistics. Or at least trying to. It's impossible to write my dissertation with . . . you know . . ." Shasta gestured in the direction of her house. "I think my adviser is about to give up on me and, honestly, I don't blame her."

"So you're seriously smart," I said, grinning. "Like one of those genius types."

Shasta shook her head. "I've just seriously done the right thing my entire life. Until I got pregnant and my boyfriend ditched me and now I'm way overdue on my dissertation. When Cornell cuts my funding I have no idea how I'm going to pay for—" Shasta took another drag on her cigarette. "There I go, getting deep again."

I downed some beer and didn't say anything.

"Where are you staying up here?" Shasta asked.

When I described my grandparents, she asked if they were that power-walk couple.

I nodded. "With the matching raingear."

"They're not exactly friendly, are they?" Shasta asked. "I've been trying to figure out whether they're racist, or just plain don't like people."

"Don't like people," I said. "With me at the top of their list."

Shasta began fiddling with her lighter and dropped it onto the deck. As she leaned over to pick it up, I noticed she was wearing a thong. Black and silky. Very hot. When she sat up again, she caught me looking. I must have flushed because as she slid back into her chair she grinned at me.

I smiled back at her. For a second, we looked each other straight in the eyes. But then there was a piercing cry from inside the house and Dewey shouted, "Mama!"

"Shoot." Shasta stubbed out her cigarette. "I better go. He gets loud quickly."

"That's cool." I drained the last of my beer.

"Listen," Shasta said, hiking up her jeans. "Dewey goes to bed around eight. Feel free to come back after that."

I nodded. "Maybe I will."

As I started down the deck, Shasta called out, "Watch out for that board."

Then she waved and headed into the house.

ten

Around nine, as Pauline and Bill were watching TV, I went upstairs and showered and shaved. I couldn't stop thinking about going to Shasta's. I wondered if she'd still have that thong on. I thought about her nipples under her shirt and what it'd be like to get my hands on them, maybe even my mouth. I'd never been with someone in her twenties, and I'd definitely never been with anyone who'd had a baby. I wondered if her body would feel different than a high school girl's, fuller or something.

At nine thirty, I could hear my grandparents pass my room on their way to the bathroom. It's the same every night. They brush their teeth together. Then the toilet flushes twice. Then their bedroom door closes.

I waited on my bed for a few minutes before heading to the door. But just as I gripped the knob, this thought flashed through my brain: *I don't want to be an asshole right now*.

There was something Shasta said earlier, *Don't let me get too deep or anything*. It reminded me of that girl, Jena, who I hooked up with at the resort last month, the one who found the suicide note. One night, when Jena and I were hanging out, she quoted a song to me about going into shallow water before you get too deep. I was thinking about Jena tonight and I kept getting a mental picture of her face the morning after I ditched her for her hot friend. I'd been heading over to the breakfast area when I spotted Jena hunched over a bowl of cereal. She looked like hell, her face blotchy, her eyes puffy. I didn't want her to tell me off, so I grabbed a banana and trucked down to the beach. But now, as I pictured her face, I realized: *I made that girl cry until her eyes were swollen*. And thinking about that, it made me feel like shit.

I let go of the knob and sank onto the bed again. I thought about that loose board on Shasta's deck and how she was on the verge of tears when she talked about it. I thought about how Shasta is a real person with real problems, and I'm just some stupid kid who got suspended from school for fighting.

Let's say I went over to Shasta's tonight and we had sex. My mom is picking me up tomorrow around lunch-time. I'm heading back to Brockport and I'll never talk to Shasta again. But she'll still be here, and she'll still be alone to handle everything, to be a single mom, to worry if she's going to run out of money. And maybe she wouldn't think about me again, either. But maybe I'd become one more thing that'd stress her out, one more thing to make her smoke and drink cold coffee.

Coach is always telling us we have to learn when to walk. I know he's talking about partying and fighting guys like Timon Birch. But right now, this thing with Shasta feels like one of those situations.

I stripped down to my T-shirt and boxers, switched off the light, and climbed into bed. I lay there for a while, my mind racing. I'm not saying it was easy, especially since I'd already gotten my head around the fact that I was going to hook up with Shasta. Those tits. That thong. Peeling off that thong. *Mmmmm.* But instead of pulling my jeans on and trekking down the lower road, I reached inside my boxers and took care of things myself. Can't hurt anyone that way. And, man, it was good.

The next morning, my grandparents went into Ithaca to do their recycling. After that, they told me, they were going to the farmer's market to get something healthy for my farewell lunch.

"Your mom looks like she needs all the vegetables she can get," Pauline said, collecting her canvas bags.

As soon as they were gone, I walked out to the shed behind the house. I found a spare two-by-four, a hammer, nails, a measuring tape, and a saw. I loaded everything into a metal toolbox, tossed in some sandpaper, and headed down the stairs toward Shasta's cabin.

Shasta was on the deck, drinking coffee and writing in a notebook. Dewey was toddling at her feet, pushing around a fire engine. When I reached the stairs, Shasta looked up.

"Hey," she said, waving. "What happened to you last night?"

"Sorry. I just didn't want to . . ." I trailed off.

Shasta studied my face for a second and then gestured to the toolbox. "What's going on with that?"

"I thought I could try to fix that board," I said, "if you still want."

"Seriously?"

I nodded. "No guarantees. I'm heading home in a few hours, but I can try until then."

"Help yourself," Shasta said.

I crouched down on the deck and got to work ripping out the rotten board. After a few minutes, Shasta scooped up Dewey and carried him inside. I'm not a carpenter, but my dad is a do-it-yourself guy and he's shown me some things. I spent the next half hour measuring the spot where the new board was going to go, sawing the replacement, sanding the edges so it wouldn't be splintery.

I was just nailing in the new board when Shasta came out on the deck.

"Where's Dewey?" I asked.

"He's watching a *Thomas* movie. My one major Mommy indulgence." She stood above me, staring down at my work. "I can't believe it."

"No big deal," I said.

I hammered in the last two nails. I was shaking the board to make sure it was secure when Shasta said, "What were you going to say before?"

"About what?"

"About why you didn't come over last night."

"I just . . ." I set down my hammer and looked up at her. "I can be an asshole sometimes and I didn't want to be one with you."

Shasta rested her hands on my shoulders for a little while and then headed back inside. As I cleaned up the scraps of wood, I could still feel where she'd touched me.

After a few minutes, I loaded up the toolbox and walked over to the sliding glass door, which was partway open. Shasta was sitting on the rocking chair, Dewey on her lap. He was drinking from a sippy cup and she was reading him a book about trains.

"All done?" she asked, looking up.

"Yeah," I said.

"Thank you so much. That was the nicest thing to do."

"It really wasn't a big deal."

Shasta and I stared at each other, neither of us saying anything. Finally, Dewey began to wiggle in her lap and point his finger down at the page.

"One second, baby," Shasta said, tousling his hair. Then she glanced back at me. "I just wanted to say that I don't think you're an—" She mouthed *asshole* over Dewey's head.

"You don't know me very well," I said.

Shasta shook her head. "I still don't think you are. I mean, we all have our moments, but don't let them define you."

"I . . ." I started. This lump was forming in my

145

throat. Goddammit. I had to split from here before I broke down.

"I better go," I said quickly, nodding my head in the direction of the road.

"Okay, well, see you around. And thanks again."

"Yeah, see you around."

I raced across the deck. As soon as I was off the steps, I could feel the tears coming on. I jogged down the road. When I reached the ravine, I chucked the toolbox and sprinted into the woods. I ran fast, hurdling over stumps, stumbling through holes.

I must have been a quarter mile into the woods when I let myself collapse onto the moss. I was breathing hard and my face was wet. As I lay on my back, staring up at the towering trees, I thought about how I didn't cry when Natalie died.

But now I was laying on the ground, twigs probing into my shoulder blades, and I was crying because Natalie and I were a shitty couple. She was most likely cheating on me. I wasn't a great boyfriend to her. If she hadn't died, we would have broken up sooner or later and we both would have moved onto better things and someday, in five years, we would have bumped into each other at a bar and joked about how we were such a shitty couple.

As it is, she's buried in Lakeview Cemetery and I've been left behind to figure it out, wonder whether I could have prevented her from dying.

Well, I couldn't. Because sometimes horrible things just happen and you have to live with the fact that there's no explanation. It is what it is. End of story.

I stayed there for a while longer, breathing in the damp leaves. And then, finally, I stood up, brushed the dirt off the back of my legs, and started out of the woods.

JUNE:
SKYE'S STORY

one

This afternoon, I asked my mom if I could give her a blowjob. She shrugged and said sure. I pressed my lips together and glanced at her crotch. We both paused for a moment. Then she tapped her script against the edge of the table, smiled at me, and said, "I think you've got it."

We'd been through the scene fifteen times already, a few where I gazed romantically into my mom's eyes and one where I flipped my hair bitchily over my shoulders. In the end, we decided this character would be all about the crotch.

It was a racy week for auditions. Earlier today, when my mom read the breakdowns that Janet emailed us, she called my manager and said, "Skye's a prostitute for one night and now everyone thinks she's a slut?"

A week ago, the independent movie I shot last fall had its television debut. I played a runaway teen who trades sex for crack. It aired on Wednesday evening in sixteen million homes and, all of a sudden, everyone and their doorman was freaking out about how they'd seen me on TV. I'd been stopped once in Starbucks, twice at the gym, and once when I was buying moisturizer at L'Occitane. People seemed surprised I wasn't wearing stiletto boots and skintight jeans. Even so, they asked for my autograph and pulled out their phones to take pictures with me.

And then, first thing this morning, Janet told us to clear the decks, that I've got two auditions tomorrow. Her assistant at Talent, Inc., emailed us the breakdowns and the sides. That's what they call scenes in the business. I was taking a shower, so my mom printed them out. I wrapped up in a towel and we read the new sides as we sat on the edge of my bed, my wet curls dripping onto my shoulders. The first audition was for a show where I'd play a boarding-school slut who goes down on every guy in New England. The other is a full-length feature by an up-and-coming writer-director. I'd heard about Pete Fesenden on the industry blogs. Everyone was saying his short swept Sundance this year. Janet told us I'd be auditioning for a lead role in his film, a fifteen-year-old girl who is having an affair with a business associate of her father's.

"Well," my mom said, rubbing my back dry with a towel.

Then she picked up the phone and called Janet. As I got dressed, they launched into this conversation about my slut potential and whether, now that I'm seventeen, it'd work to my advantage to turn up the sex appeal. I've been auditioning since I was ten and, other than the crackhead, I've always booked wholesome parts. I'm half-Brazilian and half-Caucasian, so I tend to get cast as the adorably multicultural girl-next-door. Or I guess I should say *used to* get cast. I've had a dry run for a while now, haven't gotten a serious nibble since last Thanksgiving.

I was pulling on some yoga pants when my mom motioned for me to grab my phone, that she was going to conference me in. We sat next to each other, listening, as Janet reassured us that the slut thing wasn't a trend, that she was most likely going to line up a squeaky clean audition next week. As she talked, my mom and I were nodding. We both know we can trust Janet. We've been working with Talent, Inc., since the beginning, when I was plucked out of my ballet class and invited to model.

"Skye, honey," Janet said in her hoarse smoker's voice, "these are some meaty roles."

My mom looked over at me. "What do you think?"

"They're mature," Janet said. "They have huge potential." She paused before adding, "It may be just what you need, a change of pace from the usual."

Neither my mom nor Janet said anything, but I knew they were thinking the same thing, that maybe this would get me out of my rut, keep my career from coming to a screeching halt.

"But are you comfortable doing them?" my mom finally asked.

"They sound interesting," I said. "Especially the Pete Fesenden film."

"What about you, Luce?" Janet asked my mom. "Are you okay with it?"

"If Skye's okay, I'm okay," my mom said.

"Great!" Janet said. "So call me with questions. I'm around all day. And as I said, I think this is just what Skye needs."

After we hung up, I rubbed moisturizer onto my hands and glanced out the window. It was almost nine. I could see a few younger kids scurrying across Central Park West in their plaid uniforms. It was weird to think that today was a school day, that everyone was

in class at Bentley Prep. I'd been there since kindergarten, but I left in April. If I'd stayed, I would have
gone to the prom last Saturday. As it is, I spent the
weekend at our house in Sag Harbor, where I ran on
the beach and watched movies and didn't talk to a soul
except my mom. If I don't book any big jobs, I'm set to
take the GED exam in August, which will land me with
the equivalent of a high-school diploma.

"Which one do you want to start with?" My mom set
down her phone and took a squirt of my hand cream.
"The boarding-school show or the film?"

"How about the boarding-school blowjob one," I
said drily. "We can work up to real sex by afternoon."

My mom groaned. We always practice my lines
together. Sometimes we take time to discuss the character. Other times we dive right in and then she'll give
me notes later. After seven years of auditioning, we've
done practically everything. She's confessed that she's
addicted to pain medication. I've told her to fuck herself. She's said she has two months left to live. This
winter, we had two scandalous scenes in the same
night, one where I was going to murder her and one
where she was going to murder me. After that, she
poured us some chardonnay and we collapsed onto
the couch, decompressing.

Back when I was at Bentley, my mom and I had this joke that we did sides before homework. It was sort of true. Sometimes, I'd be on my way home from school when my mom would call and say, "Janet got us an audition tomorrow morning." I'd jump in a cab and we'd spend the next few hours practicing. It's not like my mom let me slack off at school, but she never nagged me. Granted, half the time I'd be scribbling my homework assignments in the waiting room of a casting office.

"Living room in five minutes?" my mom asked, collecting the pages and heading across my room.

"Sounds good," I said.

My mom reached the doorway and then turned and studied my T-shirt and yoga pants. "If you're going to be a slut, you should dress more provocatively. Something to get you in the mood. How about that lacy camisole? And remember those red shorts you wore to the prostitute audition last fall?"

I grinned at my mom. "You *so* want my body."

My mom rolled her eyes and headed down the hall. As soon as she was gone, I turned toward my closet and let the smile slide off my face. *You so want my body*. That's something I would have said last year, and I genuinely would have laughed about it. Now I was reciting the lines, grinning the grins, but I wasn't feeling it.

What other choice did I have? I thought as I pulled off my T-shirt and wriggled into a slinky black camisole, adjusting my boobs so the right amount of cleavage was exposed. Most days it seemed like if I stopped going through the motions I was as good as dead.

In case it's not obvious, I'm one of those rich, privileged, New York City kids that the rest of the world loves to hate. I had an Italian tutor when I was two. Etiquette classes at four. Broadway dancers performing for my birthday parties and, later, professional aestheticians on hand at my sleepovers. I've always had the right clothes and the right shoes and the right friends and, basically, whatever I wanted five minutes before I wanted it.

I'm the perfect storm of overindulged offspring. I'm an only child. My mom lives off a trust fund from her oil tycoon grandfather so we have all the money in the world and she doesn't have to work to get it. And there's no boyfriend or husband to siphon away her cash or attention.

My dad died before I was born. From what my mom has told me, it was this tragically magnificent love story. His name was Andres Oliveira and he was an artist from Brazil. He came to New York for a year on a painting fellowship and my mom met him at his gallery opening. They fell in love and she got pregnant but then he went back to São Paulo and died in a motorcycle accident. All we have now are some framed photos of him around the apartment, and one of his paintings hangs in our foyer. We don't talk about him much, but sometimes I catch my mom looking at the painting and I imagine she's thinking about him, wondering how things would have been different if he'd lived. As it is, I don't know a word of Portuguese. And my only relatives are my mom's family. They live in Texas and hate the East Coast, so we have to go out there if we want to see them.

That's probably why my mom and I are so close. My acting made us even closer. For the past seven years, she's accompanied me to everything—auditions, classes, headshots, taping, more classes, more auditions, another round of headshots. In a way, acting takes over your life. All through junior high and high school, when my friends were blowing off their afternoons in Central Park, I was practicing lines, auditioning, being rejected ninety-nine percent of the time, occasionally booking a role. When I wasn't auditioning or working, I was taking singing lessons. I was doing tap and ballet and Pilates. And then, every Saturday morning, I had my on-camera class. I did that for three years, at the Ron Clarkson Studio in the west twenties. Ron's a well-known acting coach. Now I only see him one-on-one if I have a complex audition. At first, Ron had me in the teen class, then he graduated me to the adult one. Basically, it was a bunch of us sitting in a circle. We'd do scenes in front of a camcorder, and then we'd watch the footage and Ron would give us notes, how to improve our skills and how to use the camera to maximize our looks. My mom used to wait for me at a restaurant across the street from the studio. When I met her afterward, I'd be so wiped from the emotion I'd just want to sleep. Other times I'd cry the entire car ride home while she petted my hair and said, "Are you sure you want to do this?"

Of course I wanted to do it. There's no way to describe the exhilaration of being on set, all made-up and in costume, playing someone else for a few hours or days or weeks. All these directors and producers and costars cooing about how you're so beautiful and mature and talented. Not to mention that the kids at school thought the acting thing was incredibly cool. I never bragged about it, but word spread around

Bentley. I could tell in the way people were always complimenting my clothes, laughing at whatever I said. I don't want to sound pretentious, but I never had a problem making friends or getting guys interested in me.

In a nutshell, my life has been relatively perfect. Until last Christmas when, all of a sudden, it wasn't anymore.

two

By late afternoon, my mom was back on the phone with Janet. I'd memorized all my lines for tomorrow and I'd watched clips of Pete Fesenden's short on You-Tube and we'd picked out my clothes for both auditions. The casting session for the boarding-school role was at eleven in the Flatiron district and the film audition was in Tribeca at two forty-five. Now Janet and my mom were debating how I should wear my hair. I have dark brown corkscrew curls, but I can blow them out so they're straight. We debate this for every audition, whether it's a curly or straight-haired character. We even have two sets of headshots. I could overhear my mom and Janet talking. It sounded like they thought the slut would be curly, all wild and rebellious, while the girl having an affair with her dad's friend would have sleek, upper-class hair.

As the conversation lapsed into my voiceover demo tapes, I wandered into my room and closed the door. We'd been working so hard on the auditions, I hadn't had a chance to see if anyone IMed me or wrote a message on my ReaLife page. No, not just *anyone*. Matt. He was my boyfriend for almost two years. We broke up at the end of March. He still writes me occasionally. Whenever I see *Matthew Hudson* on my screen I get quivery and I wonder if this could be it, if he wants to get back together. But his notes are never more than, *Hey, Skye, what's up?* Which is typical Matt, meaninglessly friendly to everyone, the golden retriever of teenage guys.

A few people had dropped by my ReaLife page, girls from Bentley like Sophie Desmond and the twins, Bella and Drew. That used to be my posse. I guess we're still a posse, but I haven't seen them as much recently. Partially it's not being in school. But also, I haven't been in the mood for the parties and the club-hopping. The twins both wrote me today, raving about my movie and saying that everyone in school was calling me a celebrity now. Sophie tagged some prom photos for me. I checked them out and then, before I could stop myself, I jumped over to Matt's page. He hadn't put up any prom pictures yet, which is a good thing because I didn't want to see him with *her*.

I closed ReaLife and glanced out the window. Matt lives on the Upper East Side and I live on the Upper West Side. My apartment is on the eleventh floor, facing Central Park. Back when we were together, Matt used to call me when he was in the Sheep Meadow so I could look out and see him. Now the Sheep Meadow was a blur of bodies. It was a warm afternoon in early June. People were laying out in their bikinis. There were babies crawling around on the grass. On the loop, I could see runners and cyclists and horse-drawn carriages.

I opened my window a few inches, then a few more, stealing a quick glimpse at the sidewalk below. As I did, my heart thumped nervously against my chest and my stomach seized up tight. I quickly closed the window, latched it, and grabbed a pen. I jotted down a few lines and folded the paper in half. Then I changed into shorts and a jog bra, smeared sunblock on every exposed inch of my skin, and headed into the living room.

"I'm going for a run," I told my mom as I leaned over to tie my sneakers.

"Hold on," my mom said into the phone. "She's

going for a run."

There was a pause, and then my mom glanced at me. "Janet wants to know if you have sunblock on. She says they're casting fall commercials soon, so you shouldn't look too dark."

"Tell her I have sunblock on," I said. "SPF fifty."

"She has fifty on," my mom said. Then she looked up again. "And you have your phone?"

I patted my pocket.

As I headed toward the door, my mom laughed and called out, "Janet says watch for branches!"

They were referring to the time, two summers ago, when I'd landed a second callback for a Clearasil commercial. It was down to me and another girl. The afternoon before my audition, I ran too close to a tree and got a bloody gash on my cheek. All the makeup in the world couldn't hide it. Janet warned the casting people, but when I arrived at the callback everyone was still expecting me to have perfect skin. It goes without saying that the other girl booked the part.

"Tell Janet no branches," I said.

"See you soon," my mom said. "Love you."

"You too," I said.

Then I headed into the hall and hit the down button on the elevator.

* * *

My mom always says I can tell her everything, but by that she means everything *good*. The other stuff, the ugly stuff, there's not a place for that in our beautiful lives.

I never did tell her what really happened with Matt. I just said we grew apart, that it was mutual. Because to tell her about Matt would open up everything and to open up everything would mean revealing way more of the ugly than anyone wanted to hear.

The weird thing is, I can pinpoint the exact second when it started. It was Christmas last year and my mom and I were at this benefit for the Central Park Conservancy, where she's on the board. I'd been feeling off-kilter all evening, but I figured I was probably premenstrual. I was chatting with some freshman girls from Spence, and they were being all worshippy, squealing things like, *You're together with Matt Hudson! I want your life!*

That's when I saw this woman rushing around, an intern for the conservancy. She looked like she was fresh out of the suburbs, her first society event, and she was working triple-hard to fit in. Heels, mascara, the whole deal. But then I noticed this rip in the back of her dress, about two inches long. For some reason, that rip made me sad, so sad I ended up walking around the block in the freezing cold until I got over the urge to cry.

My gloominess didn't go away for all of break. It was a rainy week, so I thought maybe it was the weather. But January arrived, full of abundant sunshine, and I still felt down. It's hard to describe, except that I could see happy off in the distance, but even if I stretched my fingers really far I could never reach it.

My friends at school were like, *What's up with you? You never want to go out anymore.* My mom took me for facials and massages and even surprised me with a long weekend in South Beach. Janet was lining up auditions, but I wasn't getting as many callbacks and, even when I did, I couldn't seem to book the smallest part. I was trying harder than ever, but all the trying made me so tired I wanted to burrow in my bed and sleep.

With Matt, it was harder to pretend. It's not like we were sex maniacs, but we'd been doing it since sophomore year. Now I would cringe whenever he touched me. I just felt too removed from my body, too shut down. At first Matt was patient, but after a while he was like, *Come on, Skye, it's not like you're saving yourself.*

In late March, Matt broke up with me. Most guys would have done it a lot sooner, so that's testimony to his retriever-like devotion. I said I understood and, to be honest, part of me was relieved I wouldn't have to fend him off anymore. But then, five days later, he started going out with a blond freshman named Diana. And everywhere I looked, in every stairwell of Bentley, they were kissing and hugging and proclaiming their love.

That did me in. It got so bad that one morning I blacked out at my locker. When I came to, I was flat on the floor and the nurse was standing above me, talking to my mom on the phone. On the cab ride to my doctor's office, I told my mom I wanted to leave Bentley. I said I'd collapsed from exhaustion, that it was too much trying to juggle work and school. We know a lot of professional teen actors who are homeschooled, and we'd even discussed it as an option before. My mom agreed, as long as I got my GED and applied to colleges. The following morning, she called the headmaster and withdrew me from Bentley.

It was a relief to be away from the Matt-and-Diana show, from the daily pressure to put on a happy face, but it's not like I felt better. Mostly, I just kept waiting for the old me to return. That's why these auditions tomorrow are so important. I've decided that if I can book one of these jobs, everything might turn around. And if I can't, well, I'm not sure I can go on pretending anymore.

When I got downstairs, I waved to the doorman and jogged across Central Park West. I headed into the park near Tavern on the Green, but before I reached the running loop I dug into my pocket and pulled out the folded piece of paper. I read it one more time.

> I wonder how it would feel if I jumped. Would the sadness go away? Of course it would. I'd be splattered across the sidewalk. But do I really want to die? I guess that's the big question.

I folded up the note and dropped it on a bench. I glanced around to make sure no one saw me, then hopped over the curb and started running south. As I ran, I blasted my music and tried to focus on the rhythm of my sneakers hitting the pavement.

I ran the entire loop, all six-point-two miles of it. When I got back to Tavern on the Green, I jogged over to the bench. My note was gone. Someone found it.

They probably opened it. They probably read it.

Even though I don't know who that person is, a small part of me felt better knowing that someone out there in this world knows just how bad it can get.

three

My mom arranged for a car to chauffeur us around the city on Tuesday. The humidity skyrocketed Monday evening, so the last thing we wanted was to wind up in a sticky cab with a broken air conditioner. Two blocks into it, my hair would frizz and my nose would shine. Also, we were dealing with a tight schedule. We had to start in the Flatiron district for the boarding-school audition, complete with curls, camisole, and red lipstick. We were aiming to get out of there at noon, twelve-thirty if it dragged. My mom factored in a half hour for lunch. Then she booked an appointment at the Jon Regents Salon on Seventeenth Street to get my hair straightened. After my hair was done, I'd change into the other outfit. We went through my closet and selected a cashmere top, jeans, and low heels. Cute, yet mature. Just right for a girl who's banging a fifty-year-old man. After that, we'd hop back in the car and zip down to Tribeca.

So now all I had to do was remember my lines, look the part, act the part, and be that energetic and enthusiastic girl everyone wants.

The black Lincoln picked us up outside our building at ten. The traffic downtown was insane, so we didn't make it to Gotham Casting until almost eleven. When we stepped onto Eighteenth Street, I felt carsick. I stood on the sidewalk, attempting to swallow the nausea as my mom held out a bottle of water for me to sip.

Finally, she glanced at her watch. "Ready?"

I was still queasy, but I nodded and followed her into the lobby. I leaned against the wall of the elevator and took some shallow breaths.

We hadn't been to Gotham Casting for seven or eight months, but for a while we were coming here practically every week. As my mom secured a spot in the waiting area, I signed in. I wrote my name and Janet's contact information. That's how it works. She's the one to call us with the good news and buffer us from the rejection.

Once I was done, I glanced around the waiting area. My heart sank slightly. I hate that moment when I'm psyched for a role, lines memorized, ready to go. And then I see four or five other girls studying their scenes just like me. I always check them out and I wonder, are they more talented? Prettier? Or am I prettier? Why will one of us get the part and not the other? People are constantly telling me I'm beautiful. I used to see it, especially when I was dressed up, going out some-where. Sometimes I still do, but mostly I avoid looking into mirrors. It freaks me out to stare at myself, espe-cially my eyes, and to know all those things I've been thinking inside.

One girl was with her mom, but other than that they were alone. That's been happening more this past year, people coming to auditions by themselves, especially if they don't have to drive in from New Jersey.

As I settled onto a couch, a blond girl across from me looked up. "Skye!" she said, smiling brightly.

It was Kate Meredith, from my second year at the Ron Clarkson Studio. She's gorgeous with huge blue eyes, and she can cry on command like no one I've ever seen. We used to go out sometimes, Kate and me and a few other girls from class, to see a Broadway show or have lunch and get pedicures.

"Hey, Kate," I said. "How's it going?"

"Great," she said. "I just booked a movie. It's a romantic comedy. We start shooting in Toronto in three weeks."

"Wow," I said. "Congratulations."

"How about you? What have you been up to?"

"I had an independent film air last week," I said. "Other than that, lots of auditions. I have another one later today."

"Yeah . . . for what?"

I could feel my mom staring at me. In this business you have to keep your cards close. Next thing you know Kate, or even one of the other girls listening in, calls their agent or manager and says, "Get me a reading for the Pete Fesenden film, too."

I shrugged nonchalantly. "Nothing much. Just a student project."

"Oh," Kate said. "Well, good luck."

"You too."

"I haven't seen you out in a while," Kate added. "Have you been away?"

"Not really," I said. "Just the Hamptons."

"Listen," Kate said, "I'm getting together a group of people to see a play at the Roundabout next Saturday. Want to come? I know a guy in the cast. We can probably get backstage."

"That sounds fun," I lied. I've learned that it's better to say yes now and back out later.

"Great. I'll send you the details. Are you on ReaLife?"

I nodded, wondering how long I could keep up this conversation. It was exhausting.

"Me too," Kate said. "It's funny how—"

Just then, a youngish guy with streaked hair and wire-frame glasses came out and called Kate's name. She sprang up and followed him inside. We all sat there in silence. I read over my scenes. My mom offered me water. I read my scenes again, this time mouthing the words.

When Kate came out she was wiping her eyes. I wondered if it was from nerves or whether she'd been crying in there. I tried to visualize the scenes they were having us do. Should I have built in a good sob? Damn. Too late now.

"Skye?" the guy called out.

I handed the water to my mom and followed him inside. As I walked through the cluttered casting office, my lower lip began to quiver. A few people glanced at me and waved. I waved back, telling myself, *You are calm and relaxed. You are calm and relaxed.* And then: *Okay, Skye, if you're not calm and*

JUNE | SKYE'S STORY

relaxed, at least act like you are.

The guy with the glasses led me into the casting room. This was a first reading, so no one was there except him and April Johnson. She's a casting director I've met several times. I've had good luck with April, probably because she has this way of putting me at ease. I've booked two commercials with her and a guest spot on a sitcom.

"Nice to see you, Skye," she said, shaking my hand. "This is Maxwell. He's reading for us today."

The guy nodded as he settled into one of the chairs. I sat in the other chair, facing the camera, and placed my scenes in my lap. I memorized everything, but I still highlighted my lines in case I got lost.

"You're looking all gussied up," April said as she adjusted the camera on the tripod. "Very much the boarding-school slut."

"That's what I was going for," I said, smiling.

"Really?" April laughed. "I just thought that was your look these days."

I laughed along with her. "Oh, you know me."

April reached for the camera, but then paused. "I thought we'd start with the scene where Maggie seduces Theo, and then warm up to the confrontation one."

"Sounds good," I said, tucking the second scene under my chair.

"Before we begin," April said, "let's all shout . . . you know . . . *blowjob*." April giggled. "Just to cut the nerves. You cool with that?"

I smiled at April, took a deep breath, and shouted, "Blowjob!"

"That's my girl," April said, nodding.

"Blowjob!" Maxwell said.

"Blowjob!" April said.

My mom and I have this tradition where we don't talk when I come out of an audition. As soon as she sees me, she stands up and we walk silently to the elevator. We don't even debrief when we're in the lobby or on the street. We always wait until we're safely in the car.

After we left Gotham Casting, we slid into the Lincoln, which was idling at the curb. We were running early, so my mom instructed the driver to swing by a café for a light lunch. From there, we'd continue on to the salon. As the car pulled into traffic, my mom said, "So?"

"I think it went well. April laughed a lot. She said she liked how I did it, that I made Maggie seem more interesting."

"Great," my mom said, pulling out her phone to call Janet. "That's great."

I watched as she hit auto-dial. I knew Janet would be happy, too. Whenever a casting person uses the word *interesting*, that's a positive thing. Just like when they say you made *good choices*. The worst is when they don't comment. Just an obligatory *thanks* as you're walking out the door.

Then again, sometimes I'm totally wrong. When I think they liked me, I don't even get a callback. And when I'm completely sure I blew it, that's when I book the job.

At a little before two, we were on our way downtown. My hair was blown out. I'd changed into my jeans and cashmere top. And we even had enough time to get my makeup done at the salon. I was supposed to be playing a fifteen-year-old, so the woman didn't put on much. Just enough to accent my eyes and call attention to my lips.

The casting office of Fleming Golde Sullivan is in a tall brick building on Greenwich Street, a few blocks from the river. As I signed in, my mom took a seat in one of the chairs against the wall. There were two other girls waiting, but I didn't recognize either of them. Unlike this morning, neither of them was traditionally gorgeous. That's a difference between television and film. For TV, you have to be perfect. But films prefer quirky, more like real life. I had this urge to run into the bathroom and rinse off my makeup.

A woman in a sundress and tall boots came out and called the first girl. We watched her go in. A few minutes later, she reemerged. Two other girls arrived and signed in. I recognized one from the audition circuit and we smiled at each other. My mom began chatting with another mom, nothing personal, just summer plans and the traffic out to Long Island. The other girl was summoned. And then, finally, it was my turn.

I grabbed my scenes and a few of the curly hair headshots and followed the woman through the office. I'd been here before, but I'd never read for this casting director, Stephen Golde, one of the owners of the agency. Janet said he's a fan of my work.

When I got into the room, the woman with the tall boots sat in the reader's chair. There were two men in the other chairs. The guy closer to the tripod was older and heavyset, with a tunic shirt and salt-and-peppery hair.

"Steve Golde," he said, leaning out to shake my

hand. "This is Kara. And that's Pete. He's the writer-director."

As Kara and I greeted each other, my lip started trembling again. Janet didn't say Pete Fesenden was going to be here. It was just a reading, not a callback, so I assumed I'd be alone with the casting people.

"Hey," I said, shaking Pete's hand. He had close-set eyes and a ponytail. A white laptop was open in front of him. As I gave him a headshot, I added, "I've heard a lot about you. It's great to finally meet you in person."

"Oh," Pete said, glancing down at my picture. "Oh . . . thanks."

"Do you have any questions before we begin?" Steve asked.

I shook my head. "I'm ready anytime."

"Skye," Pete said. "That's a nice name."

"Thanks," I said, smiling widely. "My mom picked it. If I were a boy, she was still going to name me Skye, just without the e."

God, I hated this. The schmoozing part. I used to love chatting up directors, showing them how I come across in organic conversation. I could always tell they were impressed, especially when I was younger. But now it was hell. Partially I was worried that without a script in front of me I'd screw it up. Also, it was all

I could do to play one role, the one I was auditioning for. Now they were making me pull off another, the old Skye, that girl I used to be.

"Let's start with the scene where Corey meets William," Steve said. "We'll do the dad one next."

I took a deep breath. I was about to channel a fifteen-year-old seductress when Pete said, "You don't look like your headshot. You've got curly hair here."

"Yeah." I laughed lightly. "I can wear it both ways, curly and straight."

Pete glanced at my face on the monitor across the room. Generally, if I'm going to an audition with straight hair, I give the curly headshot. That way a director sees I'm versatile, that I can have several different looks. But in this case, it seemed to be confusing him, which was not the best way to begin.

Back in the car, my mom asked how it went.

"Pete Fesenden was there," I said glumly.

My mom gasped. "*Pete* was there? Janet didn't tell us that. What was he like?"

"He was okay. A little weird. He said he liked my name, but he seemed confused by my hair."

"Did he say anything else? How do you think you did?"

"He asked me to read the dad scene a second time," I said.

"He did?"

"And he gave me notes. He said to remember that I loved my father, but I was hurt by him divorcing my mom."

"Skye!" My mom reached across the seat and hugged me. "It sounds great. I think it's been a successful day all around. Maybe Janet was right. Maybe this is just what we needed to turn things around."

It did sound great. It's always good when a director wants you to read something twice. It means they want to see more. It's another thumbs-up when they give you notes, like they want to see you respond to feedback, get an indication of how you'll be on set. But even so, I felt worn out. As my mom called Janet, I leaned my head against the seat and closed my eyes.

four

Later that evening, I was soaking in the bathtub when my mom knocked on the door. I pulled the curtain closed. "Come in!"

"Are you relaxing in here?" my mom asked.

"Trying to."

"Well, you definitely deserve it after today." I could hear my mom sit down on the toilet-seat lid and begin filing her nails. "I just got off the phone with Paula Gornik. Jena is coming into the city with some of her friends on Thursday. They're seeing a show at eight, but I told Paula you'd meet them for dinner."

I groaned and slid deeper into the water. If there's one thing my mom and I don't agree on, it's Jena Gornik. Paula, Jena's mom, has been my mom's best friend since college. They sang in an a cappella group and took some wild road trip to Texas. The Gorniks are from Westchester County, an hour north of the city, so Jena and I have been forced together our whole lives.

What my mom doesn't understand is that Jena and I are opposites. She's one of those compact, bubbly types. Casting directors would call her perky. She goes to an utterly normal suburban school, the kind you see in movies, with the pep rallies and the homecoming dances and the carwashes to raise money for band uniforms. Plus, Jena lives with both her parents and her older brother who's always ragging on her but you can tell deep down he's superprotective.

Back in April, my mom went out to dinner with Paula and invited her and Jena to join us on our trip to the Caribbean the following week. When my mom informed me, I freaked out. Matt had broken up with me, I'd just dropped out of Bentley, I was feeling like hell in general—and now I had to go on vacation with Jena Gornik? I told my mom no way, she had to take it back, but by that point the Gorniks had already purchased their plane tickets and it was set.

Mostly, Jena and I avoided each other on the trip, which was fine by me. But then she started hanging out with this guy, and I hate to say it but I felt jealous. Life came so easily to her, meeting a boy on vacation, being all chatty and fun. Granted, he seemed like a total player, which I guess worked to my advantage because one day, when he and I were alone on the beach, I flirted with him and we ended up chilling for a few hours. I knew it was crappy, but I did it anyway. I just wanted to see if he'd like me more than her, or maybe I needed a post-Matt ego boost. In any case, Jena refused to talk to me for the rest of the trip. When we landed at Kennedy airport, she grabbed her bag and stormed off to meet her dad. We haven't seen each other since.

As I sat up in the bathwater, I said to my mom, "Did Jena even say she wanted to have dinner with me?"

"I think so," my mom said. "Yeah, Jena was in the background when Paula made the plans. She said Jena's going to call your cell when they arrive at Grand Central Station."

"You gave Jena my number?"

"Skye," my mom said, "please do this. Jena's grand-mother had a stroke a few weeks ago. Remember Belle? Paula says they were really close, so it's been hard for Jena. Anyway, it'd be nice for you to get out and help cheer her up."

Me cheer *her* up? Now that's funny. Jena is the queen of cheer. When we were at Paradise, Jena always carried around a quote book with that cheesy picture of the Parisian couple kissing on the cover. Once, while Jena was in the shower, I thumbed through her book. The most recent thing she'd written was *A day without sunshine is, like, night (Funniest bumper sticker ever!!!)*. I read that and I thought about how a day without sunshine is, like, my life. Which just shows how ironic it is that I'm being called upon to deliver the cheer.

My mom set the nail file on the edge of the sink. "Please, Skye?"

I scooped up some bubbles with my fingers. "Do I have any choice?"

"I booked you a table at Patsy's for five thirty on Thursday. My treat. They have to be in a cab to the show by seven fifteen."

"So the answer would be no?" I asked.

"That's my girl," my mom said, standing up.

I put my head under the water and didn't come up until she closed the door.

On Wednesday morning, I was sitting at my desk. I was supposed to be doing practice math questions for the GED exam, but instead I was cruising ReaLife. Kate had already written me about the Roundabout show. I dashed a quick response along the lines of *Oops, I forgot, I'm busy all weekend*. The twins wrote me again, complaining that I'm too far out of the social loop and insisting I go clubbing with them on Saturday night. I was like, *I'd love to but I'm really busy with an audition*. Then I checked out Matt's page. He'd posted some prom pictures with him and Diana. I stared at them a long time, hating Diana for getting him, hating myself for letting him go.

The phone rang.

"Skye?" my mom called out. "It's Janet. Pick up in your room."

I closed Matt's page and reached for the receiver.

"Skye, honey?" Janet rasped. "Luce, you're still on?"

"I'm right here," my mom said.

"I wanted to tell you both at the same time," Janet said. "I just got off the phone with Steve Golde. You got a callback for the Pete Fesenden film!"

"Really?" I asked. "Seriously?"

"A feature film," Janet gushed, "from a hot new writer-director. It sounds like Pete loved you. He said he always pictured Corey to be blond, but as soon as he saw you he decided ethnic would be perfect. Can you be there Friday at ten?"

"Mom?" I asked.

"Your day is clear," my mom said.

"Steve said they'll be doing the same scenes as yesterday," Janet said, "plus one more with the dad. My assistant just emailed it to you."

"I'm checking right now," my mom said, clicking on her keyboard.

"It's a tough one," Janet added. "Very intense. You may want to do a session with Ron Clarkson. Work out the kinks."

"I'll give him a call," my mom said.

"Keep me posted on that," Janet said.

After we hung up, I could hear my mom printing out the new scene in her office. As I waited for her to burst through my door, I wondered whether this was it. My big break. The thing that'll finally make everything better.

five

Ron couldn't see me until Thursday at noon, so my mom and I spent the next twenty-four hours practicing the new scene, getting the dry cleaner to rush back the clothes I wore on Tuesday's audition, and booking a Friday morning appointment at Jon Regents to get my hair blown out. It's an insider thing in the business that, for a callback, you should dress and look the same as you did at the audition. When I was younger, that used to be hard. My mom would have to take notes about which T-shirt I wore and whether I had on my sneakers or my school shoes.

Janet was right. The new scene was intense. It's near the end of the script, where the dad discovers that Corey has been sleeping with his business associate and he says he's disappointed in her and she tells him she's disappointed in him, too. My mom and I had been through it enough times that I'd memorized the lines, but we were struggling with how I should interpret Corey. Would she be furious or devastated? Or even ashamed? By Thursday morning, I was ready for Ron.

I took a cab to Ron's acting studio by myself. My mom was meeting someone for lunch, a woman who volunteers with her at the Met. She offered to cancel and come with me instead, but I said I was fine. It was just a matter of flagging a cab, doing the session, taking a cab home.

When I got there, Ron buzzed me in.

"Skye!" he said, stretching out his arms. He's short and muscular with a shiny bald head, like a mini version of Mr. Clean. "It was great to hear from Mom. Congrats on the Fesenden callback!"

"Thanks." I gave Ron a loose hug and an air peck on each cheek.

"So what's Pete like?" Ron asked as he led me inside. "They say he's odd, but I've yet to hear it firsthand."

I nodded. "I guess he was a little weird. He got sort of hung up on my hair."

Ron gestured for me to sit down in one of the chairs. As he reached into his fridge for a few bottles of water,

I said, "Guess who I saw at an audition the other day? Kate Meredith."

"Kate Meredith, Kate Meredith . . ." Ron handed me a water and then snapped his fingers together. "The crier! What's she up to?"

"She just got cast in a romantic comedy."

"Which one? Who's in it?"

I shrugged.

"If she didn't say anyone's attached to it," Ron said, "it's not a big deal."

I had to laugh. Ron can be snarky, but he's good. Everyone in the business knows it. Do a few sessions with Ron and you'll nail an audition.

"I'm sorry," Ron added, "but as the acting teacher Sanford Meisner once said, 'Fuck polite!'" He cracked open his water. "Now let's get started!"

The session was almost over. Ron agreed I was acing the first two scenes. The new one was tough, though. Ron definitely helped me improve it, teasing up Corey's emotion while toning down her melodrama. But something still wasn't right and we both knew it.

"What is it?" I asked, setting my notes on my lap. I'd scribbled down a lot of what he said so I could practice later.

"I'm trying to figure something out with Corey and the dad," Ron said. "It feels like you're playing her too deferential. Corey is a fifteen-year-old girl, definitely old enough to stand up to her father." Ron massaged his forehead for a minute. "Remind me about Dad. I've never met him, have I?"

"*My* dad?" I asked.

Ron nodded.

"He died before I was born," I said.

"I'm sorry to hear that," Ron said. He tossed his water bottle in the recycling bin. "What do you know about him? What did he do?"

"He was Brazilian," I said. "He was an artist. My mom met him at his gallery opening. We have pictures of him around the house. I think we look alike, except I'm lighter skinned."

"What else? What about the emotional stuff? Are you mad at him for dying?"

"*Mad* at him?" I asked, wrinkling my eyes in confusion. "He died in a motorcycle accident when my mom was still pregnant. There's not much to be mad at."

"But you've got to feel something, some sort of abandonment, something we can tap into for Corey's scene."

I shook my head. I had no idea what Ron was getting

at here, and the more he pushed the more my brain felt fuzzy.

"Well, let's run through it again," Ron said. "But I want you to think about your own dad. There are definitely some answers there." He opened another bottle of water and leveled his eyes at me. "Can I be frank, Skye? I can be frank with you, right?"

I nodded. "Of course."

"I've known you for years, and it just feels like you're missing a beat today. I'm going to need you to focus, pull your head together a little more."

I stared back at Ron, unsure how to respond.

"Cheer up, sweetie!" Ron said, drinking some water. "Now let's get you this Fesenden film."

When I got home, my mom was in the kitchen making chilled watermelon soup. She was wearing her red-and-white striped apron and she had her hair up in a ponytail. She was humming as she hacked apart a huge watermelon, pink juice trickling over the edges of the cutting board and onto the counter.

"How'd it go with Ron?" she asked, setting down the knife.

I grabbed a chunk of watermelon, took a bite, and said, "Fine, I guess. We definitely made progress on the new scene." I spit a few seeds into the trash. "He wanted to talk about my dad, though."

"Andres?" my mom asked.

I paused. "Yeah."

My mom rubbed her hands on the front of her apron. "What did he want to know?"

"He said he thought I had untapped emotion there, things that could help inform Corey's character."

My mom began chopping again.

"What was Andres like?" I asked. "I know the story of how you got together and how he was this amazing guy, but what else about him? What would he be like if I met him now?"

"He was funny and smart. He'd definitely still be painting. He had a strong accent, but his English was nearly perfect."

"What else?" I asked. "Why did he go back to Brazil when you were pregnant with me? For a visit? When was he supposed to come home?"

"The plans were a little up in the air," my mom said.

"But you were going to get married, right? What's the last thing he said to you before . . . you know . . . before he died?"

My mom collected a handful of seeds and swept

them into the trash. "On the phone or in person?"

"I don't know. Either."

She ran the water, rinsing off her hands. "He said a lot of things, Skye. I just don't know what Ron is getting at here. You've been acting for seven years. I'm sure he can help you find emotion without going into Andres."

I wandered into the foyer. There, on the wall, was the rectangular painting. It's an abstract self-portrait, a huge face surrounded by smudges of purple and black. The paint is thick in places, so the nose and chin emerge from the picture. In the bottom right corner, it says *A.O.* in tiny black letters.

I stared at the painting. Ron said there were answers here. But the problem is, I don't even know the questions.

six

I sat on my bed for a long time, mulling over the scene with Corey and her dad, thinking about what Ron said, thinking about fathers in general. I thought about my mom's dad, Grandpa Lloyd, who plays golf seven days a week and has never revealed anything personal to me in my entire life. I thought about my friends' dads, some chatty and involved, some who can never remember your name even though you've been introduced twenty times. Like Matt's dad, a big-time corporate lawyer, always wearing a slate-colored suit, always pecking away at the latest handheld device.

But what about my dad? Which cookie cutter would he have been? Would he and my mom still be together? My mom has told me that one time, as they were walking over the Brooklyn Bridge, he shouted into the wind, *I love you forever, Luce Wainscott!* So maybe they would have been. Or maybe he was just hopelessly romantic. I rolled onto my side and studied the photo of him that I brought in from the living room. He was tall with mocha skin, curly brown hair, and full lips. It looks like it was taken in Central Park. The leaves are orangish-brown, so it must have been when he first arrived in New York, the fall he met my mom. Eighteen years ago. If he lived, he'd be forty-eight now. That's so weird. I can't picture him older than thirty.

I got up from bed and went over to my computer. I logged onto ReaLife, typed "Oliveira," and hit enter. A bunch of Oliveiras popped up. Pedro Oliveira. Lila Oliveira. Francis Oliveira. And then, seventh on the list, was a guy named Andres Oliveira. When I saw that, I inhaled sharply. I peered at the small picture of this guy, smiling on some beach, all tan and buff with no shirt on. He was twenty-one, went to the University of Miami, and was originally from São Paulo, Brazil. I tapped the icon to write him a message.

> Hi,
> This is going to sound strange, but I'm looking
> for a person from São Paulo, Brazil. His name

was also Andres Oliveira. He was a painter
who came to NYC eighteen years ago. Andres
died in a motorcycle accident in São Paulo
soon after that. He was my father. I'm looking
for any information on him.
Thank you very much,
Skye Wainscott

After I clicked send, I copied the note, tweaked it a little, and sent it to all the Oliveiras on ReaLife. I'm not
sure what I was looking for, but I figured it couldn't
hurt to put it out there. I waited for a while, but no one
wrote back so I began scrolling through my friends
on ReaLife, seeing what's new. Kate was "counting
down until Toronto. Eeeeee! 16 more days!" Some girl
I went to camp with was "contemplating her ingrown
toenail." And there was Jena Gornik, "getting ready
for a big night in the city." *Oh yeah*, I thought. I was
supposed to go out to dinner with her tonight.

I opened Jena's profile. True to form, she had a quote
across the top of her page. It said: "Whether or not it
is clear to you, no doubt the universe is unfolding as it
should." Jena and her quotations usually annoyed me,
but there was something about this one that hit home.
Could it be possible that the universe, *my* universe, is

unfolding as it should and someday, somehow, every-thing will make sense? I hope so. Because I can't deal with the alternative, that life is a bunch of haphazard crap being chucked around and you just have to duck and hope too much doesn't come your way.

All of a sudden, I felt even worse for what happened at Paradise, for how I stole that guy Jena liked. I opened my desk drawer, took out a piece of paper, and wrote a note to Jena, telling her I'm sorry for being such a bitch and I hope she'll forgive me someday.

I was just licking the envelope when I heard a *ping* on ReaLife. I opened my inbox and was shocked to discover that Andres Oliveira, the one from Miami, had responded to my message.

> Hey there. I am originally from São Paulo. I have been going to college in Miami for the past two years. My mom is named Ana Oliveira. Her brother, Andres, was my uncle. I was named after him. He was a painter and I know he lived in NYC for a while, but I do not think he had any kids. When he died eighteen years ago, it wasn't an accident. I do not know how else to say this, but he was very depressed. He came home to get help and it

did not work out. I met him when I was little, but I do not remember. Sorry I could not help more. Oliveira is a common name in Brazil, so maybe it is someone else?

Andy

As I reread his message, I was trembling. It sounded like we were talking about the same Andres, especially with the painting and the timing of his death. But what was this Andy guy saying about depression and how it wasn't an accident?

I clicked print, grabbed the paper, and walked into the kitchen. My mom was standing at the counter, singing to herself as she loaded watermelon chunks into the Cuisinart. I stared at her.

My mom glanced over at me. "Everything okay?"

I stood there, not saying a word.

"Skye? Are you okay? You look like you saw a ghost."

I turned and walked back into my room. As I closed my door, I wondered how it's possible that one person's entire world can change while the other person is still making watermelon soup.

seven

I must have fallen asleep. My mom was knocking on my door. I opened my eyes and glanced at the clock. It was a little after five.

"Yeah?" I mumbled.

As my mom turned my doorknob, I flipped over the printout from Andy Oliveira. I'd been reading it when I drifted off.

"Jena just called," my mom said. "Your phone was in your bag, out in the hallway."

"What did she say?"

"She and her friends got into Grand Central Station. They're going to take the subway up here. They'll probably be at Patsy's in a half hour."

I rolled over so I was facing the window.

"You look exhausted," my mom said. "Want me to

call Jena and tell her you're not up for it? I'm sure she'll understand. You've got an important callback tomorrow."

"No, it's okay."

"Are you sure?"

"I said it's okay," I snapped. Then I got up off my bed and headed into the bathroom.

I changed into a minidress and heels. I put on eyeliner, mascara, and a touch of gloss. I rubbed pomade into the ends of my hair and swept it back from my face with a headband. I dug through my jewelry box until I found the amethyst necklace my grandmother gave me for my sixteenth birthday. I know when some people are upset they go frumpy, but I tend to take it in the other direction, doing everything possible so no one will guess I'm a wreck inside.

I grabbed the note I'd written to Jena and headed out to the living room, where I began transferring stuff from my bag into my purse.

"You look lovely," my mom said.

"Thanks."

"Are you sure you're up for this?"

I dug through my bag until I found my iPhone.

"Want me to walk you up there?" my mom asked.

"No, that's fine."

"What if you're recognized? Want to wear a hat?"

I shook my head.

"Use the Am Ex to pay for dinner," my mom said, opening the front door. "And tell Jena I said hi."

As my mom reached over to squeeze my arm, I dodged her and headed to the elevator.

On the way up Columbus, I blasted my music. I could see a few people looking at me and whispering things to their friends, but I stared straight ahead as if I didn't notice.

As I turned onto Seventy-fourth Street, I spotted Jena and two other girls waiting in front of Patsy's. I'd met them before, at a barbeque at Jena's house, but I had no idea what their names were. One was medium height with red hair. The other was tall with a black dress and dark lipstick. I took a deep breath and approached them.

"Hey, Skye," Jena said, smiling. She'd gotten her braces off since the last time I saw her. Maybe it was that, or maybe she'd grown out her hair, but she looked different, older. "You remember Ellie and Leora, right?"

"Hey," I said.

"We saw your movie last week!" Ellie squealed.

"You were amazing," Leora said. "It seemed like you really were a prostitute." She blushed a little. "In the best possible sense."

"Thanks," I said.

"I can't believe you were able to meet us," Ellie said. "You must be so busy."

"It's no big deal," I said, shrugging. "We shot it last fall."

"Shot it!" Ellie squealed. "That's such an insider's term!"

"Easy, girl," Leora said. Then she cupped her hand over Ellie's ear and whispered something.

"I'm sorry." Ellie grinned bashfully at me. "I was having a starstruck moment."

"Don't worry about it," I said, shaking my head.

I'll admit it, I used to soak up this kind of attention. These days, though, I don't deserve it. Maybe if I booked a job it'd be different, but as things are I feel like a big impostor.

We headed into Patsy's and the hostess led us to our table. After she'd handed out the menus, Ellie and Leora went in search of the bathroom. As soon as they were gone, Jena leaned toward me. "I'm not mad anymore, okay? I was really pissed about the Dakota stuff when it happened, but I'm over it." Jena brushed her hands against each other and then shook them off. "*Totally* over it."

I stared across the table at her, impressed by her level of honesty. In my world, we tiptoe around things, allude delicately to them, but never stab right at the heart.

"I . . . uhhh . . . I was going to . . ." I stumbled, reaching for my purse.

Before I could give Jena the note, she touched my arm. "I've actually learned some stuff about Dakota," she said. "Big stuff. Like, maybe it was for the best that you, well, hijacked the situation."

I set my purse back on the chair. "What stuff? How?"

"I've sort of . . . I've become friends with his brother online. I know it sounds weird and maybe it is, but you know, I really like Owen. Anyway, Dakota's in mourning. Anything with him would have been a total rebound."

"In mourning?"

"He had a girlfriend who died in a car accident a few months ago."

"Seriously?" I asked.

Jena nodded. "And she was with another guy when

she died. Messed up situation. Besides, Dakota wasn't my type. I don't know what my type is, but I've decided it's not him."

Leora and Ellie returned. We ordered a garden salad for the table and two medium pizzas, one veggie and one pepperoni. At first, Jena's friends seemed nervous around me, but by the time the salad arrived the three of them were gossiping about school and guys and summer plans. It was almost like I wasn't there. Jena tried to include me, such as telling me she's doing an internship in the city this summer, but whenever I said anything the conversation fell flat.

I started to wonder if maybe I suck at the whole talking thing. And the whole friend thing for that matter. I was watching Jena and Leora and Ellie, the way they finished each other's sentences and wiped sauce off each other's faces and constantly referred to a vast array of inside jokes. I definitely never had it like that with my friends, not even back when things were good.

I was relieved when dinner was over. I paid the bill and we maneuvered out of the restaurant and onto the sidewalk. Leora and Ellie were skipping ahead, arm in arm, toward Columbus. Jena and I trailed quietly behind.

"I'm sorry about your grandmother," I said. "My mom told me. Is she doing any better?"

Jena shook her head. "We're not sure yet. It was a major stroke, so she's still in the hospital. The doctors say it could take months or years, if ever."

"I'm really sorry."

"Thanks. It's been pretty hard."

Just as we approached the corner, I reached into my purse. "I almost forgot," I said. "I wrote you a note. It's what we were talking about before . . . about Dakota."

Jena tore open the envelope. As she began reading, her face grew pale.

"What?" I asked.

Jena opened her mouth, but then Ellie and Leora started shrieking, "Come on! We did it! We hailed our very first taxi!"

Jena started toward the cab, but then turned, stepped closer to me, and gave me a hug. I wanted to hug her back, I really did, but instead I just stood there, my arms stiff by my sides.

Dinner had been a temporary distraction, but on my way back to the apartment, it started hitting me hard. Were Andy Oliveira and I talking about the same

Andres? And, if so, did my dad really have depression? And kill himself? The more I thought about it, the worse I felt. Actually, *worse* isn't even the right word for it. I mostly felt numb, like I wasn't alive, like if a car plowed into me as I crossed the street I wouldn't feel it.

Somehow, my legs made it home. When I stepped into the apartment, my mom was at the dining-room table. I could tell by the look on her face that something was wrong. Then I glanced at the paper in front of her.

"I went into your room," she said, touching the printout from Andy Oliveira. "I was looking for the notes from Ron so we could practice tonight."

I stared at her, waiting for her to confirm whether it was true or false.

"How did you find him?" my mom asked.

So it was true.

"I did a search on ReaLife," I said.

My mom nodded.

I could feel my throat getting tight. "Was there even a motorcycle?"

"Andres was severely depressed," my mom said. "They said it was bipolar disorder. He went back to Brazil to see some top psychiatrists. He wasn't even sure he was going to return. We both decided it was for the best."

"Was there even a motorcycle?" I asked again.

"Yes," my mom said after a long pause. "But there was also a note."

I slumped against the wall. I felt like I was going to black out. "But I thought you had this great love story. When were you planning to tell me the truth? And what about the fact that I have an aunt and at least one cousin in Brazil, and they never even knew about me? How is that possible?"

"I didn't want you to be born into any more tragedy," my mom said, rubbing her temples. "Your biological father had died. That was bad enough. You didn't need to be haunted by the specific details."

"But what about me? Depression is hereditary, you know? Don't you think I should be aware of that?"

"You're nothing like Andres," my mom said.

"How do you know?"

My mom shook her head. "I know."

"Maybe you don't. Maybe there are things you don't want to see."

"Skye," my mom said. "This has nothing to do with you."

"Don't you get it?" I asked her. "This has everything to do with me."

Then I walked into my room and closed the door.

I was tossing around on my mattress, fading in and out of sleep, when my phone rattled on my bedside table. For a second I thought maybe it was Matt. He always used to text me in the middle of the night. I grabbed my cell and was surprised to see a message from Jena Gornik.

> **Jena:** I know it was you. I recognized the handwriting on your letter.
>
> **Skye:** What was me?
>
> **Jena:** I found your note at Paradise. The one by the hot tub.
>
> **Jena:** Skye? Are you still there?
>
> **Jena:** Skye? Are you getting these? Please just say something.

I turned off my phone, dropped it on the bedside table, and closed my eyes.

eight

At seven thirty the next morning, my mom came into my room with a cup of tea.

"Your hair appointment is at eight forty-five," she said as she placed the saucer on the bedside table, next to my phone. "Want me to call a car service, or should we brave it and take a cab?"

I hugged my knees against my chest. We hadn't talked since our conversation when I got home from dinner, and now she was acting like nothing had happened.

"It's probably fine to take cabs today," my mom said, lifting the dry cleaner bags off my audition clothes and laying everything across my bed. "Jon usually needs a half hour for your hair, so we'll be at the callback safely before ten."

"You can cancel it," I grumbled from my pillow.

"Cancel your callback?" my mom asked, her voice shrill.

"The hair appointment." I slid out of bed and walked toward the bathroom.

"Where are you going?"

"I'm taking a shower."

When I emerged in my towel, my mom was sitting on my bed. She'd unraveled a twisty from a hanger and was fiddling with it between her fingers.

"I can see you're upset," she said. "We had a fight, Skye. We don't usually fight, and I know this is difficult for both of us. Particularly difficult, given the subject."

I pulled the towel tighter around my chest.

"But let's put this aside," my mom said, "at least for now. Let's go to your callback and—"

"I'm going by myself."

My mom opened her mouth to say something and then closed it again, stood up, and walked out of the room. Once she was gone, I moisturized my arms and legs and got dressed. I massaged mousse into my hair, did my makeup, and headed into the kitchen for breakfast. My mom was standing over the counter, trimming stems off daisies.

"I can help you blow out your hair, if you'd like," she said.

"I'm wearing it curly."

"Didn't you say that Pete Fesenden seemed to like it better straight?" My mom gestured to the hall table, where she'd tucked a manila envelope into my bag. "You were even going to bring along the straight hair headshots. I think we all agreed that Corey isn't a curly haired character."

"Maybe she's not," I said, shaking some cereal into a bowl. "But I am."

I hopped a cab down to Tribeca. I ended up with this driver who kept jerking the brakes. When we arrived at Greenwich Street, I handed him some cash and stepped onto the sidewalk. Sweat was pooling under my arms, soaking my shirt. As I pushed through the doors into the lobby, I felt terrified. In my seven years of acting, I'd never been to an audition without my mom.

I took the elevator to the ninth floor. There were two other girls waiting in chairs, reading scenes to themselves. It was even hotter up here, and the air was still. I took a shallow breath and signed in. I was about to get the key for the bathroom when Kara came out, glanced at the sheet, and said, "Skye? Can you come with me?"

I followed her through the office. There were fans everywhere. As soon as we walked into the casting room, Kara wilted into a chair. Steve stood up, shook my hand, and said, "Thanks for coming back, Skye. Sorry about the air-conditioning. We have a guy working on it right now."

"That's fine," I said.

"You remember Pete," Steve said, gesturing across the room. Pete glanced up from his laptop and saluted me. "And this is Heather Stein. She's an executive producer on the project."

I reached over and shook hands with a woman sitting in the chair closest to me. She had glasses and brown hair looped into a bun. As I sat down across from Kara, Steve aimed the camcorder at my face.

"Anytime you're ready," he said, mopping the sweat off his forehead. "We're thinking let's start with the first scene from before and do the new one next."

I was leaning over to get the scenes out of my bag when Pete cleared his throat. "If you don't mind my asking," he said, "what's your background?"

I looked up. "My background?"

"You're half-Caucasian and half . . ."

"Brazilian," I said.

"Brazilian is good." Pete nodded at Steve and Heather. "We've already cast the dad and he's white, but we could do anything with the mom. She's a small part. Who do we know who can look Brazilian?"

As they began tossing around names, I zoned out. *My dad killed himself,* I thought. *I'd always believed it was an accident. But he wrote a note and crashed his motorcycle.* The crazy thing is, I know what he was going through, how he felt so sad he didn't think there would be an end, so numb that death didn't seem scary.

"So you're ready?" Steve asked me.

I looked up. My mouth was really parched.

"Are you okay?" Steve asked, but his voice seemed far away. "It's this heat. Would you like some water? Kara, go get some water for Skye."

Kara stood up and disappeared from the room.

"You know," Pete was saying, "I do like her hair curly. I was thinking that the other day too."

I grabbed my bag and stood up.

"You want water, right?" Steve said. "Just wait a second. Kara is getting you water."

I shook my head. "I can't do this."

And then I walked out.

By the time I hit Vestry Street, my phone was vibrating. First it was my mom. Then Talent, Inc. Then my mom again. The second time Talent, Inc., called, I picked up.

"Thank god!" Janet exhaled. "Are you okay? What happened? Did you panic?"

I didn't say anything. The sidewalk was tipping beneath my feet.

"Steve Golde called," Janet said. "He said you looked upset when you left."

I crossed Desbrosses. There was traffic everywhere. An SUV honked and swerved around me.

"Where are you?" Janet asked. "Your mom is in a cab on her way downtown. Just tell me where you are, so I can tell her."

I was halfway across Watts when my knees buckled. I wondered if I was going to faint, like I did that day at school. Somehow I made it across the street.

"Skye," Janet said, "you're having a bad day. Everyone understands that. Steve said they can see you on Monday afternoon, give you another chance."

"Forget it," I said quietly.

"What? Why? Skye, where are you? I've got your mom on hold on the other line. She's really upset. She said a friend of hers called this morning. Her daughter read something you wrote and . . . will you please just tell us where you are?"

"I'm nowhere," I said. And then I hung up.

I was on the corner of Canal, a wide, busy street. There was no crosswalk here, no traffic light. Only cars racing in and out of the Holland Tunnel. I dropped my phone in my bag and stepped off the curb.

JULY:
OWEN'S STORY

one

On the afternoon of the first day, I called my brother
and I said, "Man, you've got to save me."

"Save you from what?" Dakota asked.

I glanced around the conference room, with its plastic plants, vine-patterned carpet, and long table heaped
with Pop-Tarts, jars of Cheez Whiz, and whatever else
they thought would simulate typical teen interactions.
There were twenty of us, plus two facilitators, Jason
and Abby. As far as I could tell, they were taking their
summer jobs far too seriously.

I slid my tongue over my retainer and tried to figure
out how to convince my brother to drive two hours to
this towering hotel in downtown Syracuse. But then
Abby spotted me. She clutched her clipboard to her
chest and marched over to where I'd attempted to

camouflage myself behind a hedge of fake palm trees, which was tough given that they were five feet tall and I'm six three.

"Save you from what?" Dakota asked again.

Abby stood in front of me, tapping her toe against the carpet. During orientation, she told us she was going into her senior year at Duke, majoring in psychology, and she wanted to be a therapist someday. She was medium height, blond, and pretty in this all-American way that made my saliva evaporate whenever she looked in my direction.

"Are you still there?" Dakota asked. "What do you need me to save you from?"

Abby pointed to my phone and then held out her hand, flat and rigid like she was feeding carrots to a horse.

"Everything," I said, before clicking the end button and surrendering contact to the outside world.

"Thanks, Owen," Abby said. I watched as she wrote *Owen Evans: silver Nokia slider* on her clipboard.

I wondered how she knew my name already. Then I remembered, oh yeah, I was wearing a preprinted name tag that announced: *Hello, my name is Owen Evans. I can't wait to be your friend!* Exclamation point and all. Definitely not a proud moment in my life, but name tags were a requirement here. That, and no phones or computers. My mom actually confiscated my laptop before we got in the car.

I swallowed hard. "When can I have my phone back?"

Abby sighed. Orientation had just ended and we were having a fifteen-minute munchie break, as Jason had deemed it. A few people were talking but mostly everyone was eyeing each other cautiously, breaking corners off Pop-Tarts, submerging corn chips in fluorescent-orange cheese spread.

"This is your time to live, Owen," Abby said. "That's the point of being here. To engage, you know?"

I'll readily admit that, back home, I'm not exactly deejaying parties and scaling cliffs and living my life to the fullest every second of every day. But if and when an exciting life ever tumbles into my lap, I have a feeling it won't involve fake plants and Cheez Whiz.

"You can have your phone back on Sunday," Abby added.

Today was Thursday.

"Now," Abby said, nodding for me to come out from behind the tree, "let's go find you some friends."

* * *

221

I was in exile.

Two weeks ago, my mom took me to an Olive Garden in a strip mall. In retrospect, I should have been suspicious. My mom tends to drop bombs in public places where you can't protest at any decent decibel. Also, there's another Olive Garden in Rochester, much closer to our house. But, no, she hauled us a million miles out there. Another classic Mom move, to take you so far from home that if you needed to storm away, you wouldn't make it far. Especially if you've just turned sixteen and don't have a license and your sense of direction is only one notch up from that of an inebriated, senile, visually impaired person. Depressing, but true.

We were digging into our appetizers. My mom, perpetually on a diet, got the garden fresh salad. And I, perpetually attempting to amass body fat, ordered the Italiano sampler, a glorious mountain of deep-fried calories.

I set my retainer on a napkin next to my plate. I was just trolling a mozzarella stick through red sauce when my mom mentioned that she and some girlfriends from cardio-dance were planning a girls' trip to Key West in the middle of July. I was like fine, whatever. Ever since my parents divorced, my mom had adopted girl-speak. Friends were now *girlfriends*. Going to a movie became *girls' night out*.

As my mom raked at her lettuce, I noticed she had a guilty look on her face. I assumed she was about to tell me I'd have to stay with my dad while she was in Florida. That'd definitely suck. According to my dad, I'm a colossal disappointment. He's a Monroe County sheriff, all tough guy and scented aftershave, still riding high from his supreme jock status in high school. Varsity football, varsity wrestling, varsity baseball. And here I am, his skinny asthmatic son who flinches when someone spirals him a football, who'd rather shoot himself than go on the annual deer-hunting retreat, who works at the library, who cries at the end of movies. Not that I'd ever let my dad see the tears. He already thinks I'm a wimp. I've heard him say as much to my mom, heard him joke about my spinelessness with my brother.

At least my dad has Dakota. My older brother can bench in the triple digits. Major relief that I don't go to Brockport High School with him, that my whole life isn't, *"You're* Dakota Evans's little brother? *What happened?"* When my parents split three years ago, my mom and I moved into Rochester and she put me in an alternative school where we call teachers by their first names and do yoga instead of any sport involving a ball. Even so, I'm not exactly the center of the social hub at Alty. I have my people, a few guys, some techie girls who join our lunch table now and then. But the problem with descending from parents who were ultra-popular in high school is that they can't seem to understand why people aren't chanting my name and parading me around a football field on their shoulders.

When my mom didn't say anything, I asked, "Am I staying with Dad?"

"Your father will be on a fishing trip." She speared a cherry tomato.

"So what are you going to do? Have Dakota stay here?"

That had to be the reason my mom was looking so guilty. For most of our lives, my brother took pleasure in beating me up, usually for a wiseass remark I made at his expense. If my mom was around, she'd ground Dakota on the spot, gathering me into a hug and saying things like, "My sweet baby! Did you get hurt?" Which only made it worse because as soon as we were alone, Dakota would proclaim, *My sweet baby! My little lamb!* And then—bam!—a searing charley horse to the thigh.

But recently things have been different. It's hard

to say when it started changing exactly. Maybe when Dakota returned from my grandparents', where my parents sent him in May after he got into trouble at school. Around that time, he and my mom went to some doctors in Rochester to treat his ulcer. It was weird to find out that my brother has a bleeding stomach because I've always viewed him as invincible. After his doctor's appointments, he'd sleep over with us. And then he started coming around on weekends. Once my mom went to bed, we'd stay up together. As it got late and our eyes were glazing over from too much Coke and too many video games, he'd pull out a deck of cards and teach me some poker. I have to admit it made me feel good that he wanted to hang out with me, though I tried not to be obvious about it.

"No, you're not staying with Dakota." My mom wiped her mouth with her napkin and folded it carefully in half. "I've enrolled you in a seminar in Syracuse. That's where you'll be when I'm away."

"What are you talking about?" I asked.

"Karen at work told me about it," my mom said. "It's called ReaLife to a Real Life. They're offering it in six cities around the state this summer, but only Syracuse had openings."

I gaped at her.

"Please try to keep an open mind about this."

"Sorry," I finally said. "I meant to say, what the *hell* are you talking about?"

My mom unfolded her napkin and spread it across her lap. "Karen's daughter went over Christmas break and she's been raving about it ever since. It's for kids in your generation who spend all their time online. It'll be a chance to get away from that and really live."

"Since when did you become a self-help brochure?" I asked.

My mom ignored that remark. "You'll stay in a hotel. You'll have a roommate, but you get your own bed."

"Oh, wonderful," I said. "I'm so happy I don't have to share a bed with a strange guy."

"It's supposed to be fun. There'll be dances and a field trip to a bowling alley."

"Listen, Mom," I said, popping a fried calamari into my mouth. "I'm not going to spend the weekend in Syracuse with a bunch of losers. That's just not my style."

"So what's your style? Staring at the computer all day while everyone else your age is out in the sunshine, enjoying summer vacation?"

The way my mom described it, the teens of Rochester were doing synchronized swimming, or spinning on mountaintops, singing about how the hills are alive with the sound of music.

"I'm enjoying my summer," I said defensively. "I've seen some kids. And I've been working a lot."

"You're shelving books at the public library," my mom said, picking up her fork. "That's hardly what I'd call socializing. Owen, you're sixteen."

Owen, you're sixteen. What was *that* supposed to mean? Yet another example of the hell you have to pay when your parents were popular teenagers. It's not like I'm thrilled with the state of my social life this summer, but I was doing fine, thank you very much. I'd been hanging out with a few guys from Alty, snarfing McDonald's and talking about girls we wanted to ask out but never had the nerve. And sometimes I even had lunch with Faye, the sixty-year-old librarian where I work. Not like I'd advertise it to my mom. She'd probably find a seminar to cure me of *that* problem as well.

The crazy thing is that I'm not even a ReaLife addict. Sure, I have a page, but I hardly ever go there. What my mom doesn't know about me is that I'm a blogger. I've been doing my blog since the summer after eighth grade. So whenever she sees me at the computer and assumes I'm friending all of Monroe County, I'm most

227

likely posting on Loser with a Laptop. That's the name of my blog. Lame, I know, but I meant it to be ironic, like how people can see you for five seconds and think you're a loser but really have no idea what's going on in your head. The best part is that no one knows about my blog, not even my friends at Alty. I change all identifying names and places. That way, I can be completely honest, can say the things that get stuck in my throat in my real life.

"I've already paid for the seminar," my mom added. "It's nonrefundable."

"Maybe you should have run it by me before you wasted your money." I pushed my plate away. "I'll stay with Dakota while you're gone. Or I'm sure I can find someone else, maybe Nigel. Or Pauline and Bill. You just sent Dakota to them. Why can't I go there?"

When I said that, I could see my mom flinch. I happen to know that after Dakota got back from our grandparents' he wrote my mom an email about how he was going through some difficult stuff and it didn't help for her to ship him away, pretend he wasn't feeling things. She never would have told me about it, but I found it open on her screen one day when she was at work.

"This isn't optional, Owen," my mom said after a

moment. "July eleventh through the fourteenth, you're at that seminar."

I shoved back my chair and stormed out of the restaurant. Once I made it to the curb, I realized I didn't have my wallet. Not to mention that my retainer was still on a napkin inside. Even so, I stared at the half-empty parking lot, imagining this grand escape where I hitched a ride away from here and when my mom came out she'd be stunned to see I was gone. Then she'd learn not to register me for some stupid seminar. I mean, it's one thing for kids at school to think you're lame. But when your own mother decides your social life needs saving? Then you're really in trouble.

So here I was, two weeks later, tossing back Ritz Bits and trying not to make eye contact with anyone, lest they believed the sentiment on my name tag. *I can't wait to be your friend!* More like, I can't wait to get the hell away from all of you. Especially the guy hovering over the Chips Ahoy, humming to himself. I could hear it from the Ritz Bits—a gusty buzz, like a computer about to crash.

I hoped he didn't turn out to be my roommate.

My *god*. What had I done to deserve this? So I tend toward the quiet side. So I clam up around cute girls.

So I feel more comfortable expressing my feelings to a keyboard than a person. Does that really justify banishing me to this place, forcing me to bunk with a psychotic buzzing roommate who'll strangle me with his laptop cord in the middle of the night? Because if I get assigned to this guy, I swear that will happen.

two

Munchie break was wrapping up. As Jason solicited a few kids to help him push the food table off to one side, Abby corralled the rest of us into a wide circle on the carpet. I leaned against the wall, my knees bent in front of me, and listened as she explained how, for this activity, we had to reveal something about ourselves that no one else knows.

A girl raised her hand. She had freckles and bangs cut straight across. "No one here or no one at all?" she asked.

"No one here, Cassandra," Abby said.

"But we've just met," the girl said. "No one here knows *anything* about me."

Except that people don't need a ruler when you're around, I thought. *We can just use your bangs.*

231

"Try to think of something interesting," Abby said. "A little factoid."

"I'll go first," Jason said, squeezing in next to Abby. "I'm obsessed with table tennis."

"And I play intercollegiate field hockey," Abby said.

A guy to Abby's left said, "I love to water-ski. I may compete later this summer."

What is it about sports? Even here, in this bastion of extreme geekdom, people still need to prove they're all jocks deep down.

Cassandra said how she liked to fence and the kid next to her told everyone he's a vegetarian. And then, this small girl with reddish hair and glasses looked up for a moment. "I don't wear underwear on Thursdays," she said.

Everyone stared at her. A few kids laughed, but Abby quickly shushed the room. "This is a safe space," she said. "You can be whoever you want here."

When it was my turn, I said, "Pass."

Abby shook her head. "You have to say something."

"I did say something. I said 'pass.'"

Abby looked over at Jason. "Fair enough, dude," Jason said, shrugging. But he said it in this stiff way, like he came from another planet and read in an instruction manual that guys on Earth call each other *dude*.

When the confessions were over, Jason clapped his hands together. "So here's the deal," he said. "We'll call out two names at a time. You're going to pair off and initiate a casual conversation based on the facts that each of you just revealed."

Abby glanced at her clipboard and began reading names.

Of course, I wound up with the girl who doesn't wear underwear on Thursdays. We sat across from each other on the floor. She said "Hey" and I said "Hey" and then she began picking her fingernails. I glanced at her name tag. *Hello, my name is Julia Nicholson. I can't wait to be your friend!* My palms were clammy and my tongue was heavy in my mouth. She wasn't exactly cute. In fact, she bore a strong resemblance to a chipmunk. But she was wearing a skirt. And today was Thursday.

Abby squatted down next to us. "Hey, you two. How's it going?"

"Fine," we both said.

"Julia," Abby said, "did you ask Owen why he passed?"

Julia bit her thumbnail.

"Why'd you pass, Owen?" Abby asked me.

I stared at her. What was her deal with me? I can't

233

stand the kind of people who think the best way to summon a shy kid out of his shell is to ask him lots of questions. She probably chucks small children into deep water to teach them how to swim. Man, she was going to be one terrific therapist.

"Is it that you don't want to be here?" Abby pressed.

I shrugged. "Yeah, maybe."

"It'll get easier." Abby smiled at Julia and me. "By Saturday night you guys will be having the time of your lives."

Abby slapped me on the back so hard it made me cough, and then she ambled away. The problem is, once I start coughing I have a hard time stopping. I considered digging through my duffel for my inhaler. Always a fun moment, being the pale skinny guy with the inhaler.

Finally, I got hold of myself, and just in time because Julia was looking at me funny, almost like she was about to perform mouth-to-mouth, which would not be good given her current underwear situation.

"It's just asthma," I assured her. "I was born premature."

"Me too," she said.

The silence hung awkwardly between us, but where

were we supposed to go from here? Compare notes on our neonatal intensive care experiences?

Just then, Jason clapped his hands and announced that it was time to get our roommate assignments. He explained how we had an hour to bring our bags upstairs, relax, and get ready for dinner and the luau tonight.

Cassandra's hand shot into the air. "We're having a luau?"

"We decided on the theme at the last minute," Abby said. "But don't worry if you didn't pack any Hawaiian gear. We'll pass out flowered shirts, grass skirts, and leis after dinner."

I shuffled into line for my roommate card, silently cursing my mom for sending me to this place where it was acceptable to assume that some of us, by mere chance, brought along Hawaiian clothing. Because that's just what real life is like, after all.

I didn't get the buzzing kid, which was no small relief. My roommate turned out to be the vegetarian. John something or other. Husky Asian guy. Friendly enough. We said hi to each other and then he got on his phone. *Damn*, I thought, watching him. I was stupid to use mine in front of Abby. I mean, it was printed all over the orientation material. *No cell phones WHATSO-EVER. Turn off your phone and be present.* And my favorite: *Don't get trapped in the cell of your cell.* I assumed they were referring to prison cells and not, like, mitochondria.

After a few minutes, there was a knock on the door. John clicked off his phone and crossed the room. It was another guy from the seminar. All I knew about him was that he told everyone he once went to juvenile court for hacking into his school's network.

"What's up?" the guy said, nodding at me.

I was sitting on my bed, watching television and dealing a hand of solitaire. At least I'd thought to bring along my brother's cards, which he'd left behind the last time he stayed over. "Not much."

"You have it?" John asked him.

The other guy unzipped his hoodie and produced a slim laptop.

"Contraband computer!" John declared, pushing an extra chair toward the heavy wooden desk.

The two of them began playing a futuristic role-playing game where aliens are invading the planet. Max and Nigel, my friends from Alty, are really into that game, but I'm just not a sci-fi guy. Five minutes later, there was another knock. This time it was the water-ski kid. He cruised toward the computer and began playing, too.

I watched them for a while. Where was I when they made this plan? We were all in the same conference room this afternoon. But, as usual, I was oblivious to the cliques forming. I can't help but wonder how people pull it off. Like my brother. Our whole life, if our family went camping or to some police ball game that my dad was in, the second we got out of the car Dakota would hit the ground running with a pack of kids, leaving me stranded in the parking lot.

I scooped together my cards, dropped them in my bag, and reached for the room key.

"Where're you going?" John asked, looking over. The other guys were staring at the screen.

"Business center," I said.

"Proceed with caution, bro," John said. "Those facilitators seem hardcore."

I closed the door and headed down the long hallway toward the elevators. When I got to the third floor, I walked completely in the wrong direction, of course, before following signs to the business center. I swiped my card to unlock the door. There was no one inside, just two dingy desktops and a printer with the red light flashing, jammed paper fanning out of every crevice.

I settled into a swivel chair. As I entered the password for my blog, I immediately felt better. This was me, after all. This was home.

I started Loser with a Laptop when I was thirteen, relatively new to Rochester, and didn't have any friends yet. I wrote about missing my old bedroom and discovering which grocery stores gave free samples and how I lived in constant fear that my voice would crack. I'm sure it was boring drivel, but cathartic nonetheless. That's why I keep writing, nearly every day. Usually I write about personal stuff. Like when my brother's girlfriend was in a fatal car accident in February, I wrote a lot about that. Not that Natalie and I were best buddies, but it still shook me up. I'd never known anyone who died before, not even a grandparent.

Every now and then I get visitors. Fellow bloggers from Akron or Dallas or even Europe, telling me to *cheer up* or *keep on keeping on* or whatever emotional vitamins people shove down your throat when they think you're having a tough day. They'd usually comment for a week or two, all caring and *I'm here for you*, before vanishing into the blogosphere.

But then, in late April, Miz J left her first comment. Pretty soon, she was visiting every day. She told me she was sixteen and from a town called Topeka, north of New York City. She'd post short comments, but they were really insightful, like she was actually taking the time to think about what I was writing.

A few weeks later, Miz J asked if she could IM me. I gave her my screen name and we began chatting. She told me that her grandmother had just had a stroke and all these terrible feelings were pent up inside of her. I said I'd give her posting privileges if she wanted to blog. Later that night, she put up a post that was so heartbreaking, all about how her grandma had always encouraged her to love herself as she was, but she never really *got* it until now. After that, I said she could post anytime.

I glanced through the window of the business center to make sure Jason or Abby weren't anywhere nearby and then looked back at the screen. Sure enough, Miz J had posted a few hours ago.

> Butterflies and Dancing Stars: A Guest Blog
> from Miz J
> posted July 11 at 3:11 pm
>
> Since O Boy is in exile (a shout-out to O-Boy—
> hope you're surviving prison camp!!), I thought

I'd do a random post to fill the time until he's paroled. I don't think I've mentioned this before, but I'm spending the summer working at a children's museum. The woman I babysit for got me the internship. Four mornings a week, I take the train into Grand Central Station (all by myself!). I always stop at the same cart and get a sesame bagel. The Egyptian guy working there always says something about how if I lived in his country I'd have men falling at my feet. I smile and, for a moment, I feel all Cleopatra. (I am *so* not Cleopatra in the U.S. of A.)

But that's not what I wanted to write about. I wanted to write about the butterfly exhibit on the second floor of the museum. It's these wooden monarchs clustered on the ceiling. They have ropes dangling down from them. When you pull a rope, the butterflies flap their wings. Sometimes, on a break, I lie under the butterflies. All around me toddlers are shrieking. But somehow, in spite of the madness, I feel a sense of peace. That's the way life is, right? Chaos everywhere, but we

need to keep focusing on those butterflies
that keep us sane. Then again, as Nietzsche
said, "You need chaos in your soul to give
birth to a dancing star." So maybe the chaos
is good? After all, what girl doesn't dream of
one day pushing out a sharp, multipointed
object?

I was cracking up as I read Miz J's post. She's always funny in this self-deprecating way. Definitely my style. I went onto Instant Messenger and, sure enough, she was online.

> **O-Boy:** Cool post. Love the Nietzsche quote.
> Also, it made me think—do you know about
> the butterfly effect?
> **Miz J:** Hey, O-Boy!!! How's the slammer? I
> thought you wouldn't have a computer.
> **O-Boy:** Located one in the business center.
> Good until the wardens bust me. They've
> already confiscated my phone.
> **Miz J:** That bad?
> **O-Boy:** I have to go to a luau tonight.
> **Miz J:** Word. Have you considered a prison
> break?

O-Boy: And go where exactly? I'm in a hotel in Syracuse.

Miz J: Good point.

O-Boy: But what? You're being quiet.

Miz J: I'm just thinking about this other quote. Want to hear it?

O-Boy: Sure.

Miz J: "Break the monotony. Do something strange and extravagant!" Ralph Waldo Emerson.

O-Boy: And what does that have to do with my situation?

Miz J: You could take a bus to NYC and hang out with me. You'd be back before your mom returns from Key West.

O-Boy: And where would I stay?

Miz J: You get here. I'll figure out the rest.

O-Boy: You're joking, right?

Miz J: I guess.

Miz J: What? Now you're being quiet.

O-Boy: I'm just thinking . . .

Miz J: What?

O-Boy: Those butterflies sound cool.

Miz J: ☺

Miz J: Oh, hold on! What were you gonna say

about the butterfly effect?

O-Boy: The butterfly effect = a massive
upheaval created by a seemingly insignificant
event, like how a butterfly flapping its wings
in one part of the world can ultimately cause
a tornado on the other side of the planet.

Miz J: SO AWESOME. Where did you learn
that?

O-Boy: I work at a library. Oh, and I'm a dork.

Miz J: Libraries = good. Dorks = even better.
I think it's true, by the way.

O-Boy: What's true?

Miz J: How one little thing can set an entire
chain of events in motion.

O-Boy: Like how my blogging landed me at a
luau in Syracuse?

Miz J: Exactly. Don't get lei'd, by the way!

O-Boy: Ha.

After we signed off, I wrote a quick post, all about
the fascist facilitators and that girl who doesn't wear
underwear. But the whole time I was describing
RealLife to a Real Life, I was thinking about Miz J's
suggestion that I tunnel out of here and meet her in
New York City. Even so, I didn't mention anything

about it in my post. Maybe because I was worried she'd read it and laugh at me for taking her invitation the slightest bit seriously. Or maybe because if she commented back and said *please come*, there's a good chance I'd jump on a bus.

three

The luau took place in the same conference room we'd been in all day, except now there was a pineapple on either end of the long table. Caramel popcorn was swelling out of beach pails. And someone had positioned an inflatable tiki pole next to fake palm trees. Jason's iPod, plugged into speakers, was blasting ancient songs like "Hot Hot Hot."

To add to the humiliation of simply being here, I had to wear a yellow plastic lei. There was a sign on the door that read HAWAIIAN GARB MANDATORY—GET SWEPT AWAY BY THE TROPICAL SPIRIT. A few of the girls had grass skirts over their jeans and my roommate, John, was wearing a flowered shirt. Jason had offered Hawaiian shirts to all the guys, but John was the only taker. He also had about six leis around his neck and he was walking around saying "Aloha" to everyone as he slurped a virgin Mai Tai through a purple straw.

Abby was wearing a sheer tank top and a coconut-shell contraption over her breasts. When I first saw her, my legs went shaky. And then she, of all people, had to stroll over to me and slip on my lei. As her fingers grazed my neck, I forced myself to do geometry equations in my head. The Pythagorean theorem is the best way for me to, well, reverse the boner effect. But even as Abby toted her armful of leis to the next person and I discreetly positioned my lower half behind a table, Pythagoras wasn't pulling through. Finally, after calculating the circumference of three circles, I was back to normal.

"Hot Hot Hot" segued into ". . . Baby, One More Time." Once that finally ended, Jason paused the iPod and clapped his hands. "Hey, everyone!" he shouted. "Looks like we could use a little something to lube the conversation."

Lube the conversation? This guy was definitely not from Earth.

Abby sidled up to him. "My name isn't Abby anymore," she said. "It's *Api*. That's the Hawaiian translation."

"And I'm Iakona," Jason said.

"We looked up the Hawaiian translations of all your names," Abby said. "Are you guys ready?"

There were a few meager *uh-huh*s, but mostly no one said anything. I had to wonder whether everyone else thought this whole thing was pathetic. How could they not? Then again, some kids had actually been dancing just now.

Abby glanced at her clipboard and began reading names, pointing to each victim as she went along. Cassandra was "Kakanakala." Julie was "Kuli." Every time Abby announced a name, all the kids stared at that person. I swept my tongue over my retainer, flush against the roof of my mouth. Even here, where I didn't really care what anyone thought of me, I still detested the idea of a public gaping.

"Owen," Abby said upon arriving at me, "is *Owena*."

People looked over at me, laughing. Like, *Ha, ha, now the skinny shy kid has a girl's name, so funny*. I could feel my cheeks growing hot. I composed a mental text message to my mom, cursing her for sending me here. Seriously, is *this* what she calls enhancing my social life?

When Abby was done with the names, Jason said, "Limbo contest in ten minutes. Participation is mandatory."

He started up the music again. People meandered back to the food table. And I stood there in my yellow lei, fending off this strong sense that if I didn't escape right now, there was no hope for me ever again.

I edged out of the conference room before Jason or Abby could grab my arm and give me a lecture about mandatory fun. I hurried down the carpeted hallway and took the elevator to the third floor. There were two middle-aged men on the computers. One was checking stocks. The other was cruising profiles of single women. I noticed he had a wedding band on his left hand. *Jerk*, I thought, watching him. I wish I could find a way to email his wife and tell her what her husband really does on his business trips.

As he stood up from the computer, I shot him a poisonous glare which, judging from his boneheaded expression, he totally didn't notice. Then I sat down, logged onto my blog, and began writing.

From ReaLife to a Real Life to a REAL LIFE
posted July 11 at 8:37 pm

A few hours ago, a girl invited me to escape to New York City. She even quoted Ralph Waldo

Emerson. I've never met this girl in person, but she's read my blog so she knows more about me than anyone probably should. When she suggested the great escape—something along the lines of "stop your stupid monotony and do something cool for once" (I'm paraphrasing, sorry Ralph)—I was like, "No way could I run away from this hotel, locate a bus, and ride it halfway across the state." For one, I'm officially signed into ReaLife to a Real Life and I'm not a rule-breaking kind of guy. Like, what if they called my mom and told her I was gone? I'd be on house arrest until college, if not grad school. Also, couldn't this girl have suggested Binghamton or Albany? I've been to NYC once, when I was nine, and it was the noisiest, most crowded, and—I'll admit it—scariest place in the world. Even my dad, who as you all know can split wood with his bare hands, kept grumbling about how he should have brought his pistol.

Oh, and then there's the fact that in every story where a teenager befriends someone online and goes to meet them in person, said teen invariably ends up molested and bludgeoned. Then again, I know this girl isn't a violent criminal or a forty-year-old man. I know because . . . well . . . I don't want to go into it right now, but trust me on that one. Even so, when I got her invite, I froze in terror. Because—to put it bluntly—I'm just not the kind of guy who journeys off to meet pretty girls in big cities.

But. Yes, there's a but. Two of them actually.

But #1: I haven't been able to stop thinking about her invitation.

But #2: Maybe I don't know what kind of guy I am, after all. Or maybe just because I was a certain way for sixteen years, that can change. Look at my brother. He's definitely been changing these past few months. He said so himself last week: "It's like you wake up one morning, O, and decide that how you've been in the past doesn't have to define who you are in the future. Simple as that." I thought that was cool to hear, especially from my big bro.

All of this to say: I'll meet you there. Under the
butterflies. Tomorrow.

Before I could think twice, I clicked "post," and then
quickly checked my Buddy List. Sure enough, she was
online, but she wasn't IMing me. The guy on the other
computer glanced over. I realized I still had the lei
around my neck. I chucked it in the trash and refreshed
the screen. Still nothing. I went onto the Greyhound
site and jotted down some schedule information. I hit
"refresh" again. I looked up the address of the children's museum.

By the fifth "refresh," a new post had appeared on
my blog.

What Kind of Guy You Are: A Guest Blog from
Miz J
posted July 11 at 8:46 pm

A few hours (and nine minutes) ago, I invited a
guy to meet me in New York City. Have I mentioned I'm only sixteen and don't even live in
the city? But I invited him because sometimes
you just have a feeling about someone. Oh,
and I happen to have keys to an apartment on

Central Park West, which happens to be empty this week because the occupants happen to be in Brazil and my friend happened to mention I could crash there whenever I wanted. Okay, I'm rambling.

Back to the invite. When my grandma had a stroke in May, it propelled me into a "carpe diem" stage of life. No use muddling around waiting for life to happen, or feeling bad about myself that it's not happening. Or maybe I began carpe-dieming back in April, when I met a guy who showed me the importance of taking risks even if you fall on your face. Because that's really living, you know? So he ended up hurting me. As we all know, he was wrong for me. But I'm glad I met him because, well, it brought me here.

All of this to say I'll be under the butterflies. Tomorrow. 5 pm. (That's when I get off work.)

By the way, do you know those lines from *Juno* (best movie ever!) where the dad says to *Juno*, "I thought you were the kind of girl who knows when to say when," to which she replies, "I don't really know what kind of girl I am." That reminded me of what you said. Of course, in your case, it's guy (duh). And you're not pregnant (duh, duh). But I think it means that "who we are" can be a fluid thing, subject to change. Or maybe I'm just rambling again.

Once I was done reading her post, I could barely breathe. Not in the asthma sense. More like: *Is this really happening I think I'm turning purple what the hell have I gotten myself into I'm going to pass out.* The business guy got up and left the room. I was still struggling for air when an IM appeared on the screen.

Miz J: Are you serious? You're really going to come?

O-Boy: I'm—wheeze, wheeze—serious. You know, carpe diem and all that.

Miz J: Deep breath. Take a whiff of your inhaler. So how will you escape?

O-Boy: I'll figure something out. You really have a place we can stay tomorrow night? Who are these Brazilian people and will they kill us if we use their apartment?

Miz J: Definitely not. I helped save the
daughter's life recently so the mom is, like,
eternally grateful.

O-Boy: You WHAT?

Miz J: Long story. I'll tell you when you're
here. HERE. Oh my god!

O-Boy: Hey, how will I recognize you?

Miz J: I'll be the girl under the butterflies. If
I'm not there for some reason, just ask for
Jena. It's a small place. Someone will find me.

I took the elevator back downstairs. As I approached
the conference room, I could hear bongo drums. I
stepped inside. The lights were dimmed and they had
fake torches on the table. And there, in the center of
the room, was a hula hoop contest. A bunch of girls
were rotating hula hoops around their hips, in fierce
competition with my roommate, who now had at least
a dozen leis around his neck.

When John's hula hoop dropped to the ground, I
quickly approached him.

"What's up, bro?" he asked, wiping the sweat off his
forehead.

"Listen," I whispered. "Can I borrow your phone?
They took mine away this afternoon."

"Yeah," he said, slipping his cell into my hand. "Just be careful."

I nodded and hurried to the bathroom. As soon as I was locked in a stall, I dialed my brother's number.

"Hello?" Dakota asked.

"Hey, it's me."

"Owen? Where're you calling from?"

"My phone got taken away this afternoon. That's why I had to hang up."

"Someone took your phone away? Who? Aren't you in Rochester?"

"Mom didn't tell you?" I asked.

"Tell me what? All I know is that you called me before and said you needed to be saved. I tried you back but your phone was turned off."

I swallowed my last ounce of pride and told Dakota about ReaLife to a Real Life. When I was done talking, I braced myself for a verbal reaming, or at least a chuckle at my pathetic expense, but all he said was, "No way. No *fucking* way. What can I do?"

"Think of a reason to pick me up. I can't get out of here on my own. I need someone eighteen or over to sign me out."

"As in, dead grandmother?"

"Maybe that," I said. My throat got tight as I

wondered whether we could pull this off. "Or maybe, I don't know, I can't—"

"Don't worry," Dakota said. "I'll think of something. Do you want me to come tonight? I just have to borrow gas money."

"I can survive until morning. And I'll pay you back for gas."

"Don't worry about it. It's the least I can do. I know what it's like to be on one of Mom's exiles. And besides, I'm sort of making up for years of abuse."

"Seriously?" I asked. Dakota has never outright acknowledged our less-than-great relationship growing up. Hearing him say it now, I could feel tears stinging my eyes.

"I'm not saying you didn't deserve it, O." Dakota laughed. "But I'm restocking the karma bank and you're at the top of my list."

four

At seven thirty the next morning, the room phone rang. John was snoring like a broken muffler. I reached over to the table between us and quickly answered it.

"Is this Owen Evans?" a man's voice asked.

"Yeah," I said.

"This is Jason. I just got a call from your brother. Something's come up. A family emergency. He'll be picking you up in a half hour."

He really did it, I thought. *Leave it to Dakota.*

"Dude, are you okay?" Jason asked. "You're probably upset. Want me to send Abby over? She's good at the counseling."

"No," I said quickly, thinking of her coconut-shell bra. The last thing I needed was a boner when I was trying to look grim. "I'll be okay."

"You're a minor, so corporate is faxing me some forms for your brother to sign. That's the only way I can release you."

And my mom insisted this seminar didn't resemble any form of captivity.

"You sure you don't want to talk to Abby?" Jason asked.

"Maybe you could just ask her for my phone back," I said.

"Consider it done," Jason said. "See you in the lobby in thirty."

I took a shower and threw everything into my duffel. I slung my bag over my shoulder and turned to leave the room. John was still comatose. I wondered if he'll be weirded out to wake up and discover I'm missing. Oh, well. He seems like a social guy so I'm sure he'll survive. Then again, he was definitely nice to me, nicer than most people here. I grabbed a pen from the desk and wrote a note on the hotel stationery.

John—
I'm bailing, bro. All's fine with me despite
what J and A might say.
Take care and be well.
Peace,
Owen

* * *

When I got to the lobby, Dakota was standing by a plastic palm tree, talking to Jason. He was wearing a white baseball cap pulled low over his eyes and he had this frown on his face.

"Hey," Dakota said, holding his fist up and knocking it against mine. This is Dakota's standard greeting. It never ceases to stress me out as I struggle to remember the right way to knock him back.

"Are you hanging in there?" Jason asked.

I shrugged. I didn't know what Dakota had told him, so I didn't say a word.

"Listen," Dakota said. "We better get going. We've got a lot to do today."

Jason nodded and then handed me my phone and a blue folder. There was a sticker on it with the ReaLife to a Real Life logo. "Abby compiled some things for you," he said. "We were going to hand them out today. Dude, it's a bummer that you have to leave. If you want to call corporate, they can probably credit you for another session."

"We'll do that," Dakota said in his sincerest tone. Then he pointed his visor toward the revolving door.

I slid the folder into my duffel and followed my brother outside. As we stepped into the warm July morning, I exhaled. I hadn't even realized I'd been holding my breath.

"What did you tell him?" I asked as we crossed the parking lot, Dakota with his steady stride, and me, romping clumsily next to him. I could see my brother's car, a dented Taurus with a Brockport Blue Devils bumper sticker. Then I saw another bumper sticker next to it. A DAY WITHOUT SUNSHINE IS, LIKE, NIGHT. Weird. I gave that to him for Christmas last year. Actually, I bought one for me too, which I stuck on my laptop. I thought it was funny in a stupid kind of way. But when Dakota tore open the wrapping paper, he made this face like *more weird Owen shit* and tossed it aside.

"I called the hotel when I was about an hour away," Dakota said. "I just said there'd been a family emergency and I needed to speak to one of the leaders."

"You decided not to kill Pauline?" I asked. That's our grandmother. She surpasses all stereotypes of bitchy old lady.

Dakota smiled and shook his head. "Tempting, but as I said, I'm working on the karma thing. Besides, we sort of did have a family emergency."

"What?"

Dakota gestured his thumb over his shoulder, back

toward the hotel. "That asswipe teaching people how to socialize? Dude, that's a serious emergency."

I laughed, harder than I had in a long time.

When we got into the car, Dakota offered me a can of Coke and a pack of Nutter Butters. "Breakfast?"

"Thanks," I said, tearing open the cookies.

"I figured you'd be hungry."

Dakota started the car. Classic rock blasted from the sound system, the bass pumped high. I studied my brother as he glanced in his rearview and shifted the car into reverse. Sometimes I can't believe he's only two years older than me. He seems so confident, driving all the way to Syracuse, taking care of business. Even when I'm eighteen, I doubt I'll have caught up with Dakota.

"You want to go to Rochester or Brockport?" Dakota switched on his blinker. "I'm thinking Brockport is probably safer. Mom won't have any scouts reporting to her. When she gets back from Florida, we can just say you got sick and I picked you up and we didn't want to bother her while she was on vacation."

"Actually . . ." I spit my retainer into my hand, ate a Nutter Butter, and drank some Coke. "Would you be able to take me to the Syracuse bus station? I looked it up. It's on the P and C Parkway, off Route Eighty-one."

Dakota turned to me. "Why are you going to the bus

station? I can drive you home."

"I'm not going home," I said quickly. "I'm taking a ten-twenty-five bus to New York City."

"Why the fuck are you going to New York City?"

"To see a girl." I ate another cookie and tried to look as casual as possible.

Dakota stared straight ahead, one hand gripping the wheel. *He's angry*, I thought to myself. *He thinks I've trapped him into this, used him to sign those release forms. In a way, I guess I did.* I wondered if Dakota was going to yell or, worse, smack the side of my head. I clutched my hand nervously over my gut. I suddenly had to pee.

Dakota turned to me. "So who's the girl? Do you even know her?"

"Yeah," I said vaguely. "I know her."

Dakota drove down the highway in silence. After a minute, he glanced at me again. "Is she hot?"

I nearly choked on a Nutter Butter. "Yeah," I said. "She's also nice."

Dakota ate two of his cookies and then said, "But here's the problem. Mom would kill me if she found out. You know that, right? She'd kill *me*, not you. I signed those forms. I drove you to the goddamn bus station."

"I think I'm more on the line here," I said.

"You don't understand," Dakota said. "Let's put aside any sibling shit right now and lay it all on the table. You're Mom's baby. If anything happened to you, my ass would be so far on the line there wouldn't be any room left for your skinny ass."

I stared out my window, picturing Jena waiting for me under the butterflies, wondering why I hadn't shown up. Or maybe she knew I wouldn't show. She's read my blog, after all. She knows I'm a chicken.

"How important is this?" Dakota asked.

I turned to him. "Very."

"So give me the details."

I told him how I'd go to New York City today and meet up with her. We'd already arranged a time and place, and I had plenty of cash from my library job to take cabs everywhere. She had keys to an apartment where we could sleep tonight. Tomorrow morning, I'd catch a bus back to Rochester. I'd only be gone thirty hours, but it'd probably be the most significant thirty hours of my life.

When I said that, Dakota nodded. "Tell me where it is again."

"The bus station?" I asked.

"Yeah."

I dug into my pocket and pulled out the map I drew from the computer last night. Dakota glanced over at it. Then he veered off at the next exit and did a quick U-turn in a parking lot.

Once we were back on the highway, this time heading in the opposite direction, Dakota turned to me. "I have to say, you blew me away just now."

"What do you mean?"

"Maybe because you're my little brother, but I just didn't think that was your style, running away to New York City to meet a cute girl. It's pretty legendary." Dakota popped a Nutter Butter and shook his head. "Blew me away."

"Thanks, I guess," I said. I was trying to sound low-key, but in reality I was swelling with a near-explosive amount of pride. Our whole lives, my brother has never, ever given me that kind of compliment.

"I've met a girl, too," Dakota said after a minute.

"Oh, really?" I asked sarcastically. I mean, it's not exactly a newsflash that Dakota has met a girl.

"I know, you're so surprised. But this one is different. First of all, I can't even call her a girl. She's in her twenties and has a little kid. And are you really ready to be blown away?"

I nodded curiously.

"It's a platonic deal. We're just friends and we want to keep it that way. We've been writing letters back and forth. She lives up near Pauline and Bill. That's where I met her."

"Letters?" I asked.

"Like with an envelope and a stamp."

"I'm blown away," I said. "I'm so far up in the sky the birds can't even reach me."

We both cracked up. A little while later, as Dakota pulled into the bus station, he shifted into park. "I'm going to wait with you."

"You don't have to," I said.

"I want to make sure you get on that bus."

He reached for his door handle and then paused, leaned across me, and clicked open the glove box. He scrounged around for a second before producing two condoms. "Take these with you," he said, tossing them into my lap.

I stared at the orange wrappers. They were extralarge condoms. Dual pleasure. My face flushed. Extra large and dual pleasure are two things I can honestly say I've never experienced in my life.

"I don't think I'm going to need these," I mumbled.

"Take them." Dakota slugged me in the arm. "The last thing we need is another little you running around."

As Dakota stepped out of the car, I sat there for a second, rubbing where he punched me. Some things never change. *Then again,* I thought as I tucked the condoms into my bag, *I guess other things do.*

five

At ten thirty, the bus rolled out of the Syracuse station. I settled into a window seat near the middle, far enough from the bulk of people in the front, but not too close to the reeking toilet. I set my bag on the neighboring seat, mainly to detract anyone from plopping down next to me and telling me their life story for five hours. I put on my iPod, circled through until I found my mellowest playlist, and attempted to relax.

That lasted exactly four minutes.

As we accelerated along the highway, I could feel tightness creeping into my chest. Had I really just said good-bye to my brother and boarded a bus to New York City? I can chat online until the cows jump over the moon, but when it comes to actually *talking* to a girl, I can barely string together a pronoun and a verb.

I reached into my bag and pulled out that ReaLife to a Real Life folder. On the right, Abby stuck in today's agenda. On the other side of the folder, there was a worksheet labeled *Conversation Starters: Tips and Topics*. I quickly scanned the page, which included pointers like "Try to discover things you have in common." Below that, they had sample icebreakers.

- Can you recommend a great pizza place?
- What's the last movie you saw?
- If you could time travel, what era would you go back to?

When I got to the time-travel question, I shoved the worksheet into the mesh holder behind the seat in front of me. Like I was about to tell a girl that I wanted to drift down the Mississippi River with Huck Finn or see a play performed at an amphitheater in ancient Rome. *Right.* That'd do wonders for me.

Full admission here. Miz J's real name is Jena Gornik and she once hooked up with my brother. She revealed that in one of her first IMs. She started it just that way.

In the interest of full admission, she wrote, *there's*

something relatively huge I've got to tell you.

I assumed she was going to say her real name was Jim and she was a middle-aged pedophile.

I'm bracing myself, I wrote back to her.

That's when she told me she'd seen me in real life before.

When she said that, I was shocked and slightly terrified. What if she went to Alty? If that was the case, I'd never set foot in my school again.

What??? I nervously typed. *Where?*

She went on to tell me that she saw me at Paradise, the vacation-from-hell my mom took my brother and me on over spring break. It was a few months after Dakota's girlfriend died, so you couldn't say anything to him without him snapping at you. He and my mom fought all the time. The first day, when I pulled on my khaki shorts, Dakota suggested taking me over to the health club and getting my skeleton legs started on the five-pound weights. After that, I spent the week in jeans. I mostly slept and posted on my blog and tried to steer clear of his path of destruction.

Deep sigh, Jena wrote before admitting that, while at Paradise, she'd fooled around with my brother.

I didn't say anything for the longest time. I just sat there, hunched over my keyboard, feeling like a big loser for assuming she'd found my blog randomly and had connected with my words. Because that's what the past few weeks had felt like, ever since her first comment. Especially since we'd started IMing the day before, it was like we understood each other on some deeper level. But no. It was about Dakota. Of course it was about Dakota. Even when he's at his worst, he manages to charm the ladies. Seriously. Wherever we go, girls are flirting with him, or trying to chat me up so they can gain access to my brother.

Will you still talk to me? Jena finally asked.

Sure, whatever, I wrote. I wasn't about to tell her I was crushed or anything. Just to drive home the point, I added, *So I guess you want info on Dakota?*

At first I did, Jena said. *But then I realized that . . . can I be honest with you?*

Fine with me, I wrote. What did I have to lose? I was just the news source for my brother. Nothing more, nothing less.

Dakota hurt me, Jena wrote. *He didn't treat me well, though it took me a little while to realize that. I originally went onto your blog to find out more about him (call me a stalker), but then I read your posts (all of them, even from 2 years ago!) and you showed me what a decent guy is really like. And now with everything going on with my grandma . . . I don't regret what happened with Dakota, but I'm completely over it. I just wanted you to know that.*

I read and reread her message before finally writing, *How did he hurt you?*

For one, he ditched me for another girl. But also, he didn't respect me. He treated me like an object, not a person with feelings. I'm sorry. I know he's your brother, but you said I could be honest.

No, that's fine, I wrote back. *You've read my blog. You know he's treated me that way too.*

So you'll still talk to me? You're not just saying that?

Yeah, I will. I paused before adding, *But can I ask you a question?*

Of course.

How did you find me? Does Dakota know about my blog? At that point, in late May, the prospect of Dakota reading my personal thoughts sent me into a sheer panic.

He never mentioned it, Jena said. Then she explained how, even before she'd met my brother, she saw me in the business center at the resort one night and glimpsed the name "Loser with a Laptop." When she said that, I tried to remember a girl coming into that room, the only place that had wireless. I knew from the picture on her ReaLife page that she had brown eyes and medium-length brown hair. But no, all I could remember was this one housekeeper who barged in and yelled at me in Spanish to move it so she could sweep. Jena said that when she saw me that night, I was listening to music and pounding furiously at my keyboard. She'd stood behind me, wishing she could tap my shoulder and ask if I wanted to hang out, but I didn't look up so Jena eventually left the room.

I wish I'd looked up, I wrote to her. *If I did, though, I probably would have been too chicken to take you up on your offer.*

Or maybe not, Jena said. *Maybe we would have stayed up for hours having an amazing conversation and telling each other things we'd never say in the daylight.*

I guess that sums up why I'm going to New York City. I want to look up this time. I want a second shot at that conversation.

I slept for most of the ride. At some point, I opened my eyes and the bus was speeding past hills and lopsided, peeling barns. An hour or so later, we pulled into a small city with low brick buildings. A woman with two young children got off. A guy with long hair and a backpack got on.

As we got closer to New York City, traffic slowed to a crawl. The driver announced we'd be getting to the Port Authority Bus Terminal a half hour late, around four. Everyone immediately got on their phones and reported the delay. I didn't have Jena's number. Last night, when we were IMing, we decided to do it the old-fashioned way where people promise to be somewhere and actually show up. I guess if it got really late I could look up the number of her museum.

As I stared out the window at the jumble of cars and trucks, I thought about how when Jena first told me she'd hooked up with my brother, I felt completely insecure. I mean, how could I ever live up to *that*? But then, as we continued chatting, I really did believe her when she said she wasn't the same girl she'd been back in April. Over the past month, we've even talked about Dakota, like how his girlfriend's death messed him up. In June, when I blogged that Dakota was acting nicer to me, more human, Jena commented that she was genuinely happy. But it wasn't like, *Oh, goodie, maybe I'll get another chance with him*. It was more like she was happy because her brother meant a lot to her and everyone deserves a good sibling.

As the bus picked up speed again, I wondered if I'm not the same person I was before, either. Like Dakota calling me legendary and giving me two of his freak-ing condoms. That *never* would have happened two months ago.

A few minutes later, the bus entered a long tunnel, which I assumed was going under the Hudson River. When we emerged on the other side we were in New York City. There were skyscrapers everywhere, so tall the streets were shadowy. The driver maneuvered through some crowded streets before pulling into a massive, several-story garage and shutting off the engine.

"Port Authority!" he called out.

People stood up and collected their things. Well, everyone except me. I huddled in my seat, unable to move. *What the hell was I doing here?* I asked myself. *Was I really about to step off this bus and onto the side-walks of New York City all by myself? Was I insane?*

"You getting off?" the driver called back to me.

I nodded up at him and said, "Yeah."

I was here because I wanted to be here, I told myself. *And, yes, I was going to venture into New York City by myself. And maybe I was insane, but it was better than the alternative, hiding behind my laptop instead of liv-ing my life.*

And so I reached for my duffel and walked slowly down the narrow aisle.

six

As I wandered aimlessly through the Port Authority Bus Terminal, my pep talk to myself disappeared into thin air. Or more like smoggy, unbreathable air. Honestly, I felt like hell. My boxers were bunched around my balls and there was a rank ripeness radiating from my armpits. I kept searching for a sign, any sign, telling me where to go next. Dakota had instructed me to look out for a taxi area, that that's what he and his wrestling team did when they came down to the city a few years ago. But all I could see was this massive crowd of people jostling each other and shouting into their phones. And there were so many smells—bus exhaust and incense and who knows what else. It was so strong my lungs were constricting. I dodged into the nearest men's room and reached into my bag for my inhaler.

The bathroom was grimy, one faucet dripping and a fluorescent light flickering on and off. A few guys were lined up at the urinals. I had to pee, but I had no interest in a public display, so I closed myself in a stall. I hung my bag on the hook, shook my inhaler, and popped off the cap. I exhaled, closed my lips around the mouthpiece, and pressed down. As I kicked up the toilet seat with my sneaker, I could feel the medicine working its way through my body. I hate the way it makes me feel, jittery and anxious, but it's better than not being able to breathe.

I flushed the toilet, and then stripped off my T-shirt and bunched it into my bag. I slid on a fresh layer of deodorant, dug around for a new shirt, and unlocked the stall. There was only one guy out there now, swishing with mouthwash. As I washed my hands, I glanced at my reflection in the mirror. Skinny with messy reddish hair, jeans, and a gray T-shirt. It was hot today, probably eighty-five. I thought about changing into shorts, but then I remembered Dakota's comment about my skeletal legs. Besides, I don't have tons of leg hair yet, and what I do have is this annoyingly invisible shade of pale orange. No, shorts are definitely *not* the way to go if I want to make any kind of first impression with Jena.

After I left the bathroom, I bought a bag of chips and a water from a guy in a magazine stand. As I was tucking my wallet back in my jeans, I suddenly got paranoid that someone was going to pickpocket me. I remember when we came to New York City before, my dad kept talking about how there are thieves everywhere and you have to know what to do when a man holds a gun in your face and demands your money. My heart, already racing from the medication, began thumping even harder.

"You okay?" asked the guy at the magazine stand. He was a tall African man with a gap between his front teeth and deep scars down his cheeks.

"I'm just . . . I'm looking for where to get a cab," I said.

He pointed to an exit door ten or fifteen feet away, then smiled and said, "You'll be fine. You'll be okay."

I wondered how bad I looked. My dad always says it's important to appear confident even when you're scared shitless, that people smell vulnerability and will prey on it. But it's one thing when, like my dad, you lift weights, wear a uniform, and pack a pistol. It's another thing when you're, well, me.

Somehow I found the cab line. I was standing in

front of three women with streaked hair and too much eye shadow. They kept talking about the Broadway show they were going to see on their girls' night out. When I heard that, I thought of my mom on her girls' trip and I had a flash of terror about what she would do if she knew where I was right now.

"You're up!" the taxi dispatcher barked, pointing at me.

I approached the nearest cab, opened the back door, and climbed onto the seat. The driver had a phone clipped to his ear and he was talking, loud and fast, to someone in a language I didn't recognize. I sat there, waiting, unsure what to do.

"Where to?" the driver asked.

"Uh, the Children's Museum?"

The driver said something into his phone and then glanced over his shoulder at me. "What are the cross streets?"

I fumbled in my pocket for the piece of paper. "Two-twelve West Eighty-third Street."

"Between?"

"Uh . . ."

The cab behind us honked. My driver clicked on the meter and the car lurched forward.

* * *

Twenty minutes later, we arrived in front of a tall stone building. There was a blue awning out front that said CHILDREN'S MUSEUM OF MANHATTAN. I handed some cash to the driver, grabbed my bag, and stepped onto the street. As I did, I thought, *See, look at me doing this, all confident and cool, just like I belong.* I slung my duffel over my shoulder and I swear I could feel new muscles in my forearm.

But then, the second the cab pulled away, I wanted to flail my arms and say, *No, come back! You're my last connection to, I don't know, the bus station that contains the bus that could zoom me back to the comfort of my home.* I watched miserably as the bright yellow car disappeared down the block.

Now I was alone on a sidewalk in New York City. Alone with four pigeons, three kids on scooters, a couple going at it under some scaffolding, and a guy in a necktie droning into his cell phone, "I understand where you're coming from. I really do. I can see it in your eyes." *No, you idiot,* I wanted to tell him. *No, you can't.*

I stared up at the Children's Museum. I couldn't believe Jena was inside at this very moment. My stomach flipped excitedly as I glanced at my phone. 4:57 P.M. *Now or never, O-Boy. Now or never.*

I walked up the ramp and into the lobby. Moms and dads and babysitters were wrestling kids into strollers, dragging them toward the door, chasing them with juice boxes. I cut through the crowd and approached the ticket counter.

"Can I help you?" asked a middle-aged woman behind the desk. Her hair was pulled back with a red scarf and she was wearing a name tag that said *Rosie*.

"I'm . . ." I glanced at the price to get in. Jena hadn't mentioned whether I should pay or just explain that I was meeting up with her.

She tipped her head to one side. "Are you here for Jena?"

"Yeah, I'm Owen."

"Well, go on upstairs!" she said, smiling. "Jena's on the second floor. She said you'll know where to find her."

She handed me a sticker and instructed me to put it on my shirt. It was a picture of a unicorn which, at the end of the day, is an improvement over *Hello, my name is Owen Evans. I can't wait to be your friend!*

I headed up the stairs. On the first landing, a sandy-haired toddler was spread-eagle on the ground. His dad was standing above him, waiting. When I reached the second floor, I headed down a short hallway, turned the corner, and glanced into a huge room.

I spotted Jena right away. She was laying on the floor, staring upward, her arms at her sides. I was partially obscured behind the doorway so I watched her for a second. She was wearing cropped pants and a blue T-shirt that said INTERN. She looked different than her ReaLife picture, younger, even prettier. No, not just prettier. As my brother would put it, Jena was hot.

Forget about flailing. Now I was completely drowned.

I turned abruptly and raced toward a bathroom. There were arrows everywhere, but I kept getting lost and winding up surrounded by packs of wailing babies. When I finally locked myself in a stall, I was gasping. But it wasn't asthma. Now it was full-fledged panic. Who was I kidding? There's no way I was going to be able to hang out with this girl. It's one thing to IM her, to craft these smart messages that crack her up. But it's another thing entirely to be here, in person, trying to be someone I'm not. This is Dakota's kind of girl, after all. I'm in way over my head.

I grabbed the condoms out of my bag, chucked them in the toilet, and flushed. One went down, but the other burped back up. I flushed again and they were both gone. I could feel tears coming on. I wiped my eyes with the back of my hand and thought about how much I'd been hiding in bathrooms recently. Yesterday at the hotel, Port Authority, now here. I could envision the post I'd write when I got back to Rochester. *The Stall Report*. All about how I traveled to New York City to meet a girl but ended up cowering in toilet stalls instead.

I pictured Jena reading it, realizing I came this close and stood her up. *No,* I thought. I couldn't do that to her. She was here. She came. Even if I was a spineless wimp, it still wasn't okay to hurt her like that.

I headed back downstairs. This time, I walked right over to her, dropped my duffel on the ground, and said, "Hey."

"Owen," she said. "You made it!"

Her eyes were hazel and sparkly with long, dark lashes. I never noticed that in her picture. In fact, I thought her eyes were brown.

Jena patted the carpet next to her. "You should lie down. Look up at this."

I lowered myself onto the ground and stared at the butterflies. Jena tugged one of the ropes and they flapped their orange wings. We were laying so close, our shoulders were touching. And then, at the exact same second, we turned our heads and looked at each other. She smiled, revealing a silver-colored retainer. I flashed my retainer back at her.

"Matching retainers!" she squealed.

I laughed, but didn't say anything. I suddenly felt very thirsty. And hungry. And happy to be here.

*s*even

"Want to get out of here?" Jena asked after a little while.

I nodded, and we both stood up. Another thing I hadn't realized from her pictures is that she was short. I was a giant, nearly a foot taller than her. I slumped my shoulders. There are guys who carry their height, big quarterback bruisers named Hunter or Mark, but I don't feel like I've earned my inches. They're just something that happened to me.

"I have to run up to the office and grab my backpack," Jena said when we reached the stairwell. "Want to wait here?"

"Sure," I said, leaning against the railing.

As I watched her go, I thought: *What the hell am I doing here?*

No, I knew what I was doing here. I'd been through that enough today. Now it was more like: *Okay, I'm here, but what the hell am I going to say?*

I wondered what Dakota would say in a situation like this. Hold on, he *was* in a situation like this. I wondered how he acted around Jena. I bet he was sarcastic. That's how he gets around cute girls. With his old girlfriend, Natalie, they were always arguing and making fun of each other. My mom used to say that she couldn't tell whether it was love or hate. I bet my brother called Jena *babe*. I bet he made some comment about her breasts. There's no way I could pull off something like that. Not that I even wanted to.

I was feeling a stab of jealousy that my brother and Jena had hooked up when I quickly reminded myself that she didn't want to be with someone like Dakota now. She'd made that point very clear. She didn't like how he treated her. She could never be herself around him. No, Jena was here because she wanted to be with me, because she felt like we had a connection.

"Ready?" Jena smiled as she hopped off the bottom step. She'd changed into a white shirt with tiny buttons at the neck and she had a backpack strapped over her shoulders.

We walked in silence down the next flight of stairs.

As we headed through the lobby, we passed the woman at the ticket counter. She looked like she was shutting down for the night.

"Hey, Rosie," Jena said, waving. "This is Owen."

Rosie smiled at me. "Where are you kids headed?"

"We haven't figured it out yet. Maybe food?" Jena touched my arm. "What do you think?"

"Uh," I said. All I could think about was Jena's hand resting on my arm.

"You're working tomorrow?" Rosie asked Jena.

"Yeah," Jena said. "At ten."

We waved good-bye. Jena and I pushed through the doors.

"We don't have to get food," Jena said as we headed down the ramp. "I just said that. We can do anything."

"No, food sounds good."

"What do you want?"

"Anything's fine," I said.

"How about pizza? There's a good pizza place around the corner."

"Pizza's fine."

"I can't stand when people say fine," Jena said. "I never know if they're saying fine like *great*, they're craving pizza more than anything in the world, or fine like they'd really rather have Mexican or Chinese."

"Pizza's great," I said.

Jena smiled. "Better than anything in the world?"

I nodded and shifted my duffel on my shoulder. By this point, my mouth was so dry I could barely swallow.

We took a left on a street called Amsterdam. Jena steered us into a tiny pizza parlor. It was just big enough for the counter, two wobbly tables, and a trash can.

"Supposedly it's the best pizza in New York City," she said, approaching the counter. "I come here for lunch. It's cheap, too."

Jena ordered a slice of cheese. I got two pepperoni, garlic knots, and a large Coke. I hadn't eaten anything today except the Nutter Butters and the chips, and I was starving.

We carried our trays to the nearest table. I dropped my duffel by my feet. Jena put her backpack on the seat next to me.

"I'm sorry for my rant before, about the word 'fine,'" she said as she doused her pizza with parmesan. "I was trying to be funny, but it came out the wrong way. I'm an idiot sometimes, especially when I'm nervous."

Jena took a bite, chewed slowly, and then said, "It's weird, right? In some ways I feel like I know you so well, and you know so many things about me."

I downed a garlic knot. The obvious subtext here was: *But in person, we're not bursting with chemistry.* I wanted to make us burst with chemistry. Believe me, I did. But the problem was, I didn't know how.

Jena sighed heavily. "I can't believe you came. I told my parents I was sleeping over with this girl, another intern at the museum. I stay there sometimes when I have to work early the next morning. What about you? Did you escape okay?"

"Dakota picked me up," I said, drinking some Coke.

"Really?"

"Yeah."

Neither of us said anything. I glanced at Jena's face to see if she was pining for my brother or wincing in pain upon hearing his name, but she just took another bite of pizza and wiped her lips with a napkin.

"I really can't believe you came," Jena said.

"Me either."

Jena studied my face. "You look different from last time. I guess I only saw your profile, but you still look different."

I was wondering whether Jena was implying different *good* or different *bad* when she smiled at me. I mean *really* smiled where she tipped her head to one side and her eyes crinkled a little around the edges. I almost started to feel relaxed, but then I remembered that Jena had keys to an apartment, that that's where we were staying tonight, and I thought, *No way*. No way. There's no way I can go from never having kissed a girl to sleeping over with her in an empty apartment.

Forget about drowning. Now I was submerged in the sludge with the crustaceans and the medieval shipwrecks.

After we finished our food, we popped in our retainers and walked toward Central Park. Jena led the way since, as usual, I had no sense of north, east, south, or west. As we paused at a traffic light, Jena suggested we hop a cab to the apartment and drop off my bag.

My stomach flipped at the mention of the empty apartment.

"That's okay," I said casually. "It's not too heavy."

In reality, it was ripping my muscle from my bone, but I was hardly ready to be alone with her. No, seriously, I'd rather dislocate my shoulder than have her staring into my eyes, waiting for me to sweep her into some passionate embrace of which I'm completely incapable.

"We can take turns carrying it if you want," Jena said.

"No, it's fine."

"Fine?" Jena asked, making a face.

"I mean, it's great," I said. "I want to carry this bag more than anything in the world."

Jena cracked up in an adorably girly way where she closed her eyes and covered her mouth with her hand. Watching her, I had to smile. I couldn't believe I'd made her laugh like that.

We crossed another street and there was Central Park. I'd seen it in movies but I'd never been inside before. Of course I hadn't. The last time I came to New York City my parents got into a huge argument because my mom wanted to take a carriage ride through the park but my dad said no way, that it was "a festering cesspool of crime." Those exact words. But as Jena and I stepped through the stone gate and into the park, all I could see were trees and lawns and paths and playgrounds. It was six twenty and the park was full of bikers and runners, children squealing in water fountains, people sitting on benches reading the newspaper. No cesspool. No crime, at least not at this hour.

As we wandered down a narrow path, Jena did most of the talking, with me murmuring the occasional *Wow* and *Cool* and *Really?* so I didn't come across as a total mute. She explained that she walked in Central Park during her breaks from the museum. She told me about her best friends, Ellie and Leora. She pointed out a guy riding his bike with huge speakers strapped to the back, blaring music.

Sometimes, when it got quiet, I scrambled to think of something to say, but my mind kept drawing a blank. I thought about that icebreaker worksheet from ReaLife to a Real Life, how it said we're supposed to find common ground, like foods we crave and movies we've watched. I even considered bringing up the subject of time travel. That's how desperate I was.

"Want to hear something my grandma once told me?" Jena asked.

We were at the top of the Reservoir, looking at the shimmering water and the Manhattan skyline off in the distance. It was impressive, the sweeping kind of view that almost makes you feel like you could do anything. Almost.

"The one who had a stroke?" I asked.

Jena nodded. "It was when she was visiting us for Hanukkah last year. My parents were out somewhere, shopping I think, and we were baking cookies and talking about how she met my grandfather. He died a long time ago, before I was born. Anyway, she basically told me that I'll know I've met the right person when I'm comfortable being quiet around him."

I looked over at Jena, wondering where she was headed with this.

"Not like I'm supposed to shut up all the time, but you've probably noticed how I have a hard time with silence."

"I don't mind."

"But I do. Sometimes I just want to *be*. Like how you do it."

I stared at Jena. Did she really think I was just *being*?

"I like how you are," I mumbled, staring into the water. My cheeks burned as I said it. I kept my eyes fixed on a bloated stick floating a few feet out.

"Really? You really do?" Jena asked. "Well, I like how you are too."

It was all I could do not to collapse on the gravel path in total disbelief.

* * *

We continued walking around the Reservoir. The sky was a darker blue, and there were runners everywhere, snorting like warthogs. Now and then, we'd smile at each other and bump our arms together. Something had changed between us, a certain barrier broken down. It was subtle, but I think we both knew it had happened.

Which is why it was really odd timing to get a text message from Dakota. But there it was, vibrating in my pocket.

Yo, did you make it to the Big A? Dakota wrote. *What time are you coming back 2morrow?*

I quickly typed, *i'm here & all is cool. i'll call you from the bus* and then tucked my phone back in my jeans.

"Who was it?" Jena asked.

"Dakota," I said. "Just making sure I'm okay. See what I mean? He's become a different person recently."

"He wouldn't have done that before?"

"Definitely not." I shook my head emphatically. "And want to hear something crazy? He told me this morning that he's met a girl—"

"That doesn't seem too crazy," Jena piped in.

"But it's just platonic. They're, like, writing letters back and forth."

293

"Letters?" Jena asked, laughing.

"That's exactly what I said."

We headed down a path and through a pine grove. There were people everywhere, all walking in the same direction, carrying grocery bags and pizza boxes and picnic baskets.

"They're going to the Great Lawn," Jena said as we approached. "They have free symphonies and operas in the summer. I heard some moms talking about it at the museum. Today is the New York Philharmonic. Want to check it out?"

"If my brother is writing letters," I said, "I can go to a symphony."

Jena giggled like she had before, with her hand over her mouth. I swear, she was making me feel like a comedian. It was awesome.

We followed the crowd over to the Great Lawn. There must have been thousands of men and women sprawled on blankets, drinking wine, lighting candles, breaking baguettes. They were facing a wide stage where an orchestra was playing classical music.

"I can't believe so many people come out like this," I said. "That's so cool."

"I was thinking the same thing," Jena said. "It's nothing like my town."

"Mine either."

"I want this when I get older," Jena added. "Everyone hanging out and listening to Puccini together. How many people in this country want to do that? Probably not so many. Most people probably think it's dorky when they could be, like, at a tailgate party. But if you get a huge group together and they're all doing something, that thing becomes normal. Does that make any sense or should I shut up right now?"

"No, I definitely get it," I said. And I did. In fact, for the first time in my life I was witnessing a scene I could envision being part of. It was also making me think about ReaLife to a Real Life and all those synthetic attempts to get us to socialize. From what Jena said, I guess the concept of the seminar looks good on paper—a group of dorks, free from any outside scrutiny, having the time of our lives. But the truth is, it has to happen naturally and it's going to be different for every person. And, in my case, it's definitely not going to include a limbo contest.

We headed over to a grassy spot under a tree. I tossed down my duffel, massaging the painful grooves in my shoulder. Jena pulled a sweatshirt out of her backpack and spread it out for us. We sat down and lay back with our heads on my bag.

I was listening to the music and attempting to appear relaxed, but mostly I was thinking, *Holy shit Jena is so close to me right now holy shit.* Literally, her face was three inches from my face. Her hair, which was splayed across my bag, was touching my neck. And then there were her hands, resting across her belly. Whenever I glanced at her hands, my stomach clenched up and I'd launch into another round of holy shits.

"I meant what I said before," Jena whispered, "about the silences."

I stared up at an airplane's lights flickering across the sky. "But don't you want that guy from my blog? All talkative and stuff?"

"You *are* that person. It's just another side of you." Jena paused before adding, "I recently copied down this quote. It was from the person who's supposedly the founder of blogging, like a million years ago. He blogged all through college but then quit to actually live his life. He said that intimacy can happen in quiet moments, that it doesn't always have to be about words."

Her hand was so close. Holy shit. I could reach over and hold it. Holy shit. But how exactly do you hold someone's hand without making it seem like you're grabbing it, stealing it away from them? And why was my hand suddenly so sticky? Holy shit.

"What is it with you and quotes?" I asked, wiping my palm on my jeans. "You know so many of them."

"I used to think I collected quotes because I had no life, so I had to feed off other people's," Jena said. "But now I've realized I like them because they make me feel less alone. Like we're all going through stuff and we can share our wisdom with each other. I don't know. I guess quotes make me feel more connected."

"Like we're all in this together?" I asked.

"Exactly," Jena said.

Maybe it was the warm night. Or maybe I was emboldened by the darkness. Whatever it was, I reached over and took Jena's hand. Her fingers felt slender and soft. We stayed that way for the rest of the concert. When the music was over, there were fireworks over the stage, massive explosions of blue and white and orange. Everyone else clapped, but Jena and I didn't let go of each other.

eight

When the concert was over, Jena and I followed the herd of people out of Central Park. It was too crowded to hold hands, but whenever I thought about how it had felt, I got this goofy smile on my face. But it was okay because a few times I looked over at Jena and she was smiling, too.

Jena mentioned that the apartment where we were staying was on Central Park West, about ten or fifteen blocks down. We could either walk or catch a cab. The sidewalks were flooded with people scrambling for cabs, so we crossed the street and began walking.

"It's weird to have keys to someone's apartment," Jena said as we waited for the light to change.

"You said something about saving the daughter's life?" I asked.

"It's a sad story," Jena said, sighing heavily. "Do you really want to hear it?"

I shrugged. "We've got a ways to walk. And my bag is crazy heavy. May as well distract me while I'm carrying it."

"I thought you said the bag wasn't so bad," Jena said.

The walk sign flashed and we stepped into the street.

I cleared my throat. "I was trying to impress you, I guess."

"It worked," Jena said, grinning.

"So tell me how you were a superhero."

"Not a superhero really." Jena stepped up on the curb. "Do you remember Skye? That girl I went to Paradise with?"

I nodded. It'd be hard not to remember Skye. She was superskinny and overly put together, like she was obsessed with her appearance. Maybe it's just me, but I'm not attracted to girls who look like they're anorexic. Even if I did recognize her from some TV commercials and everyone at the resort was whispering about how she was famous. Naturally, Dakota found a way to meet her. One evening, when my mom told me that the movie-star girl was coming with us to see a phosphorescent bay, I faked a stomachache. Or maybe the stomachache was real because as soon as I considered the prospect of being in a car with her, I thought I might puke.

What I later learned, from Jena, is that Skye was the one my brother ditched her for. Which seems like a bad call on Dakota's part. But I guess a good thing in the end because otherwise I probably wouldn't be here.

"We're staying at Skye's apartment," Jena said.

My cheek twitched nervously. "She's not going to be there, right?"

"No . . . why?"

"She's just kind of scary."

"She's actually not so bad," Jena said. And then she went on to tell me this story about how she had discovered a note Skye had written about wanting to kill herself. It was at Paradise, the night Jena met my brother. She didn't recognize the handwriting, though, until a few weeks ago when Skye gave her a letter. Jena freaked out and texted Skye, who didn't deny the suicide note. After agonizing about it all night, Jena told her mom, in case Skye was a threat to herself. Jena's mom told Skye's mom, who sort of knew Skye was depressed but wasn't willing to admit it. But upon

hearing the suicide stuff, she rushed Skye to a therapist and got her on medication and supposedly she's
already doing better.

"Basically," Jena said, "Skye's mom is forever grateful to me. She gave me a copy of their keys and said I
could crash at their apartment during my lunch break
if I wanted. But then Skye separately told me I should
come here when they're in Brazil."

"What are they doing in Brazil again?" I asked. "I
thought she was in the middle of a breakdown."

"Skye's dad was Brazilian," Jena said. "He died
before she was born. They're down there meeting his
family this week. Skye said it's part of her healing pro-
cess."

Just then, Jena stopped in front of a broad building with a forest-green awning that stretched over the
sidewalk. "Here we are," she sang.

I stared up at the imposing facade, my feet unable
to move.

"Coming in?" Jena asked.

"Oh, you know," I said, my tongue growing drier by
the second. "Maybe I'll stay out for a little while and
sleep on one of those benches over there." I gestured
across the street toward Central Park.

Jena laughed. "That's called homeless, Owen."

"I'm not the most . . ." I paused, wiping my palms on my jeans. It felt like every droplet of saliva in my mouth was leaking out through my hands. "I'm not the most, you know, experienced person in the world."

"Like I am," Jena said. "I have an idea. How about we agree to leave the lights off when we get upstairs? It'll be just like Central Park. Except there won't be fifty thousand people with us."

"Can we at least invite two or three?"

"Come on." Jena grabbed my hand and dragged me into the marble lobby. She waved at the doorman, who greeted her back. She stepped into the elevator, pushing the button for the eleventh floor. I shuffled in after her.

It was the longest elevator ride in the history of the universe. Both of us stared up at the display, watching the floors slowly go by.

We finally arrived on eleven. Jena unlocked the door, swung it open, and we stepped into the foyer. It was relatively dark, but I could see the outline of a large painting hanging on the far wall. It was this scary-looking face, frowning and haunted, with a nose protruding from the picture. I shivered briefly and then glanced into the shadowy living room, where there was a grand piano, white sectional couches, and delicate glass vases on every surface.

"People actually live here?" I whispered to Jena.

"Let's go to Skye's room," she said. "It's a little more normal in there."

We tiptoed down a hallway and into a room on the left. There were windows overlooking Central Park and the New York skyline. As Jena disappeared into the bathroom, I did a quick visual inventory. Fluffy double bed. Desk. Two wide dressers. Definitely more normal. Then again, Skye lives here, which makes it slightly intimidating. But she's in Brazil, I told myself, nearly five thousand miles from here.

Jena emerged from the bathroom, slid her feet out of her sandals, and climbed up on the edge of the bed, looking out the window. I wriggled out of my sneakers and sat next to her.

"Can you believe this view?" she asked.

I shook my head. "I want to live in New York City someday. Maybe I'll apply to college here."

"I've been thinking the same thing," Jena said.

Jena looked over at me and smiled. I smiled back at her, my hands trembling, my teeth chattering. I swear, there must have been a fault line inside my body.

"I'm glad the lights are out," Jena said.

"It reminds me of this study I once read at the library."

"Where you work?"

I nodded and told her about how these psychologists studied a bunch of college students who didn't know each other. They put some of them in a lighted room and some in a dark room, and then watched to see what would happen. The people in the room with the lights on made small talk and acted uptight, but the people in the dark were, basically, all over each other.

"Like how?" Jena asked.

"Everything," I said. "They were hugging and laying in each other's laps and some were even, you know, kissing. The researchers concluded that people feel less inhibited in the dark."

"That's so amazing," Jena said.

"What? That I'm a dork who recites studies from old psychology textbooks?"

Jena giggled and shook her head. "No, about the dark. It reminds me of blogging, like how you feel comfortable revealing personal stuff when you don't have to see the people who are reading it, when it's more anonymous. That's definitely how I feel."

"I guess you're right," I said.

"Then again," Jena said, "with blogging you can't do this."

Before I knew what was happening, Jena pulled my face toward her and kissed me. We kept our lips pressed together for the longest time, just breathing each other in.

"Uh, Owen?" Jena finally asked.

"Yeah?"

"Do you think we should, uh, take our retainers out?"

I had to smile. "What would your orthodontist say?"

"Definitely not."

"Mine too."

We chucked our retainers onto the bedside table and began kissing again, with our tongues this time. Jena moved closer to me. As I felt her breasts against my chest, I immediately started getting a boner. I wondered if I should do geometry equations or whether I should just let things happen. I traced my hand down Jena's body, feeling her amazing curves, and thought, *Screw the Pythagorean theorem.*

After a few minutes, Jena whispered, "What are you thinking?"

"I'm just really liking this."

"Me too." Jena paused before adding, "Can I ask you something?"

"Yeah, of course."

"Is it okay if we take things slow? Maybe save some stuff for next time?"

"Uh, yeah. Definitely."

"Good."

Jena rested her head on my shoulder and I put my arm around her.

"Owen?"

"Yeah?"

"Thanks for coming. It's the most romantic thing anyone has ever done for me."

I squeezed her even closer. I wanted to thank her also, but I could barely speak. My eyes were stinging because all I could think about was that Jena said she wanted to save stuff for next time. *Next time*. She'd met me. She'd spent a whole evening with me. And she still wanted a next time.

nine

When I woke up the next morning, my left arm was tingling. I could barely feel my fingers. Jena was asleep next to me, her cheeks flushed, her lips turned up in a sleepy smile. The sun was coming over the buildings, a fresh golden light glinting across Central Park.

I slid my arm out from under Jena's neck. As I shook my hand around, I thought about how you haven't really lived until you've woken up in a strange bed at sunrise with your arm around a beautiful girl. In a few hours, this bubble will inevitably burst. I will take a cab to Port Authority and suck on my inhaler as I wait for the bus to Rochester. Jena will go to the Children's Museum and stack blocks and hand out tissues and try to find peace among the chaos. I'll call Dakota from the bus station. Maybe he'll tell me that my mom got wind of my wanderings and is flying back from Florida ready to chew me to shreds. Maybe I want that to happen. Maybe it's time for me to stand up to my mom, for her to see me as something other than her premature baby who needs to be protected, needs to be saved.

Maybe when I board the bus, I'll decide not to put my duffel on the neighboring seat. Maybe I'll tuck it up above instead so that someone can sit next to me. When the person begins telling me their life story, maybe I won't reach for my iPod. Maybe I'll decide I have a life story, too, and I'll reveal some of it.

But for now, nothing has to happen. For now, I can just be here in this strange bed at sunrise. And so I slipped my arm under Jena's neck again and fell back to sleep.

acknowledgments

Thank you to:

My editor, Tara Weikum,

for plunging into these characters with me.

The whole team at HarperTeen for their enthusiasm for
Tangled, and that great butterfly display.

Jocelyn Davies, for always being so helpful.

Deborah Noyes Wayshak, who was there at the beginning.

Rachel Vail, Megan McCafferty, and Wendy Mass,

for knowing just what it's like.

My research helpers, Kathy Jaccarino, Tom Manjarres, and
every teenager who ever shared a bit of their life with me.

My mom's group, Sarah Torretta Klock, Melissa van Twest,
and Jhoanna Robledo, whose support sustains me.

Magda Lendzion, for taking such loving care of my little guy.

My parents, Anne Dalton and Ian Mackler,
for still answering the phone at any hour.

And Jonas and Miles Rideout,
who I love with everything I've got.

tangled

My Life Story

I was born in Manhattan on Friday, July 13, 1973. When I was one, my parents moved us from Greenwich Village to Syracuse and then to Brockport, a small village in western New York (and the setting for many of my novels and stories). I did K-12 at Brockport Central School District. Things were okay from kindergarten through fourth grade, when I lived in a creative oblivion—building tree forts, riding my bike, and starting a newspaper with my best friend.

From the beginning, I loved to read and write. When I was four, I would tell stories into a tape recorder (I still have the tapes!). I also dictated stories to my mom. She'd write down my words, I'd color the pictures, and then she'd stitch them together. I read obsessively. My first real chapter book was *The Wizard of Oz* by L. Frank Baum. From there, I read every book I could get my hands on—the Beverly Cleary books, the Judy Blume books, *The Great Gilly Hopkins*, *Tuck Everlasting*, *The Witch of Blackbird Pond*, *The Girl with the Silver Eyes*, *Homecoming*, the Great Brain books. Often I occupied those worlds more than my own. But it was okay. In elementary school, people didn't catch on that I lived in fiction more than reality.

In fifth grade, everything changed. I was going through a phase of wearing plaid boarding-school dresses, my hair in long braids and ribbons. But suddenly, as if there were a special summit to which I was not invited, the other girls started wearing cute lavender tops, designer jeans, and feathered hair. I was still playing with dolls—and they were gossiping, whispering, and clustering together in the school yard. It was official: I was a misfit.

Needless to say, junior high sucked. It helped that my parents loved me even though sometimes, at home, I wore a straw flowerpot on my head. Also, I had a best friend, Stephie, who lived three doors down. Stephie is a year younger than me, so we weren't together in school. But the second we got home, we were inseparable. We played violin. We wrote notes on balloons and released them in a giant field near our houses. We took vacations with each other's families. Sometimes, on warm summer mornings, I'd carry my cereal through the two backyards separating our houses, and Stephie and I would eat breakfast together. Even though my school life was stressful, my home life was happy, much thanks to Stephie's friendship.

Things got better in high school. Stephie started hanging around with some boys. That meant, by default, I got to hang around them, too. My parents took me on a shopping trip and I picked out clothes that might help me fit in a little better. I joined ski club. I got my first boyfriend. I became obsessed with George Michael's *Faith* album. I started assembling a group of friends and, at some point along the way, my confidence bounced back from its junior-high low. Sophomore year, I made friends with Jen, who had long blond hair and drove a black Trans Am. Senior year, I met a wannabe rock star on an airplane and he wrote a song for me. I got cast in the school musical. I fell in love for the first time and, yes, I had my heart broken for the first time, too.

Even so, I was still haunted by feelings of being a misfit. While things looked okay on the surface, I often felt like no one really understood what was going on in my head. That's where I turned to young adult novels. I read and reread all the Judy Blume books. I read *A Summer to Die* so many times I can still remember passages by heart. I devoured every other book by Lois Lowry. I loved the M. E. Kerr books because the characters often seemed so alone and I could relate to that. And the Norma Klein books. And every other YA novel I could find in the Seymour Library.

People often ask me now why I write novels for teenagers. Lots of reasons. One of the biggest reasons is that I honestly believe that, along with certain friendships, I was saved by the books I read during those years. They spoke to me in a way that nothing else did. They helped me feel less alone. They made me laugh. They made me see there was a world bigger than my high school.

15 Things You Never Knew About Carolyn Mackler

Birthday: July 13, 1973

Hometown: Brockport, NY

Adopted Hometown: New York City

Family: My husband, Jonas, and our two young sons. My huge assortment of parents, stepparents, stepsiblings, parents-in-law, stepparents-in-law. And, of course, my friends, who are family to me.

Favorite Color: Blue, all shades

Biggest Quirks: I'm a picky eater. I've been a vegetarian since I was four. I frequently joke to my husband that I'll eat anything as long as it doesn't include meat, fish, or goat cheese.

Favorite Savories: Potato chips and onion dip. Southwest sourdough bread, toasted with butter. Cheese fries. Popcorn. Definitely popcorn!

Favorite Sweets: Chocolate (the darker, the better). Elephant ears. Strawberry shortcake. Fresh raspberries by the gallon.

Favorite Things To Do: Spend time with my husband and sons, read novels, write novels, ride my bike, walk in Central

Park, swim in lakes (not in Central Park), eat sweets and savories, take road trips in the summertime.

Favorite Movies: *Juno, Funny People, The Kids Are All Right, A Walk on the Moon, Love Actually, The Graduate, Garden State, Annie Hall, When Harry Met Sally, You've Got Mail.*

Favorite Books: *This Lullaby, Summer Sisters, Forever . . . , Gingerbread, Thirteen Reasons Why, Looking for Alaska, America, Boy Meets Boy, Rats Saw God, Hard Love,* The Jessica Darling books (*Sloppy Firsts, Second Helpings*), *Stargirl, Elsewhere,* the Harry Potter books, *A Summer to Die, Caucasia, Shopgirl, A Tree Grows in Brooklyn, Marjorie Morningstar.*

Celebrity Crush: Adam Sandler (yes, I like funny guys)

Inappropriately Young Celebrity Crush: Michael Cera (so cute!)

Inappropriately Old Celebrity Crush: Dustin Hoffman (have you ever seen *The Graduate*?)

Real-Life Crush: My husband, Jonas

You Asked, Carolyn Answers: Questions About *Tangled*, Writing, and Censorship

Which of the four narrators in *Tangled* is most like you?
Some days I'd say Jena. Other days I'd say Owen. I suppose I'm more of the observer type than the life of the party. Then again, of all the stories, I loved writing Dakota's the most. I have a tender spot for him and his struggles. And for Skye as well. There are bits of me in all four of them. I have to have that in order to relate to a character.

While writing *Tangled*, how did you get into the head of a teenage boy?
It was definitely an interesting challenge. Owen was easier . . . but Dakota! How was I, a non-wrestler, non-jock, going to write about Dakota? I knew him, so capturing his voice and his feelings weren't hard. But how could I do the sports stuff? Early into the first draft of *Tangled*, I was speaking at a school in suburban Chicago and I mentioned my dilemma to a crowd of juniors and seniors. Afterward, I was approached by a senior guy, Tom, who said he was a wrestler and would be happy to help. We exchanged information and set up a phone call. He definitely wasn't Dakota—he was very sweet and humble—but he was a trove of information about wrestling, working out, guys' feelings about their biceps. Tom even helped me choreograph Dakota's fight with Timon outside the auditorium!

How did you pick the title for *Tangled*?
I wanted a title that showed how Jena's, Dakota's, Skye's, and Owen's lives are all entwined. For a while, I had *You, Me, Her, and That Loser with the Laptop*, but it was too wordy. Maybe even too negative. I also wanted the title to reflect the things I

was thinking about as I wrote this book, about how our worlds are all tangled together, and how what you do can affect someone else, even if you don't know it. So I was keeping a long list of title ideas and nothing was clicking. Then, one day, I was at the library and I scribbled down, *Tangled Up in Each Other*. That same day, in a stroke of wild coincidence, my editor emailed me and said, "How about *Tangled Up in You*?" And then my agent suggested shortening it to *Tangled*. It was a definite collaboration, a tangled-up collaboration.

Have you always wanted to be a writer?

I've always loved telling stories. As I got older, I began writing in my journal. I was usually making lists of all the guys I was lusting after and ranking my likelihood of ever going out with them. By the time I hit college, I began writing poetry and short stories. That's around the time I realized how much I needed to get out the stories that were inside my head. Pretty soon after I graduated from college, I wrote an early draft of *Love and Other Four-Letter Words*.

Do you write every day?

When I'm working on a novel, I write almost every day. Even if it's just for a few hours, it keeps the momentum going in my head. I do my best writing in the morning, right after consuming a cup of strong coffee. I don't allow myself to write at night or else I can't fall asleep. I'd lie in bed for hours, thinking, *Who are these characters? What motivates them? What will happen next???*

I want to write a novel. Any advice?

I have a speech I love to give called "Carolyn's Top Ten for

Aspiring Novelists." I'll do a "Five Greatest Hits" version of it here:

1. Write. Write what you love. Write what makes you excited. Be honest. Don't be shy about putting in whatever you want (you can always edit later).

2. Read. Read current books in the genre in which you want to write. Read about the marketplace. If you're writing for children or teens, check out the *Children's Writer's & Illustrator's Market*. I found it very helpful when I was starting out.

3. Don't Show Anyone. In Stephen King's smart memoir *On Writing*, he says to write your first draft with the study door closed. I love that advice. It helps so much to keep the story in your head during that first draft, to let it be in a world all yours, without positive or negative input from anyone.

4. Show Select People. Once you're finished with a draft, get out there and talk with other aspiring authors. Take a class in novel writing. Join a writers group. If you're writing for children or teens, check out The Society of Children's Book Writers & Illustrators. They have hundreds of regional conferences (plus a great national conference) that will connect you with authors, agents, editors, and fellow aspiring novelists.

5. Throw Out, Revise, Start Over. My agent, Jodi Reamer, always says that the strength of an author is in her/his ability to rewrite. That's definitely true for me. I've thrown away thousands of pages (and a few entire novels). While it's painful in the moment, my books are always better for it.

Where do you live?
I live in Manhattan. My home is on the eighth floor of an apartment building. I look out over rooftops and sky.

Where did you grow up?
I grew up in a small village in western New York called Brockport. It's near Rochester, near Lake Ontario, a few hours away from Niagara Falls. When I need a town for a book or short story, I often write about Brockport. I've lived in Manhattan for most of my adult life, so Brockport is the only town I know intimately. But even though Brockport is real, all my characters in it are made up.

***The Earth, My Butt, and Other Big Round Things* is on the ALA Office of Intellectual Freedom's list of most challenged books of 2006 and 2009. Were you surprised? What is it like to be the author of a banned book?**
I'm not surprised to be on those lists because *The Earth, My Butt, and Other Big Round Things* has many instances of being banned around the country, most notably in a school district in Carroll County, Maryland, where 350 teenagers signed a petition demanding the book's placement back in their high school. Then again, I'm incredibly surprised *The Earth, My Butt, and Other Big Round Things* is the subject of so much controversy.

I wrote a book about a plus-sized girl who learns to feel happy in her skin without having to lose weight or do damaging things to her body. Ever since this book's publication, I've received hundreds of letters from teen girls telling me that *The Earth, My Butt, and Other Big Round Things* has helped them feel good about themselves, be more confident, and stand up to people who treat them badly. With a message like that, who would want to keep this book from teen girls?

I find book banning very frustrating because, even if parents decide a book is not right for their child, they should not be allowed to keep it from every other teenager in town.

A book is being banned in my school or library. What can I do to stop this?

The first step is NOT being quiet about it. It is NOT okay to remove books from libraries and schools, so please don't let it happen without a protest. Even if it's a book you can't stand, you still want to protest it—it may be *your* favorite author next! It can be hard to protest a book banning by yourself, so talk to friends about it, and gather a group of people who all want to protest together. Here are some things to do for starters:

Go to the American Library Association Office of Intellectual Freedom website. They have extensive resources on what to do if a book is being challenged. And be sure to report the challenge to them—they collect this information and use it to keep books in schools. Also, visit the National Coalition Against Censorship website. There's a button on the right where you can report a book challenge. They've also created a wonderful tool kit for handling book censorship in schools.

Report the challenges to your local newspapers. There are so many people who will work to keep books in schools. Your job is to make sure we find out about it. Good luck!

What are you doing now? Are you writing another book?

I've just written a collaborative novel with Jay Asher, the author of *Thirteen Reasons Why*. It's the story of two teenagers, Josh and Emma, who are next-door neighbors and formerly best friends. It takes place in 1996, at the cusp of the internet revolution. Emma is installing AOL on her new computer when something funky occurs and she's granted access to a website that hasn't been invented yet: Facebook. She drags Josh over and they slowly realize they can see information about their lives fifteen years in the future, but only in small snippets, one status update at a time. As they begin reacting to this new-found knowledge, they notice changes to their adult selves on Facebook, which causes even more drama in the present.

This was an amazing book to write—both because of the concept and the ease at which the story came about. But mostly, it was having such a talented collaborator. It goes without saying that writing novels is an isolating profession, and I spend more time in my head than I care to admit. But with this book, I never felt alone. If I was stuck on a character or a scene, or I wanted to share a funny idea, I could send an email to Jay because he knew this imagined world as much as I did. (And sometimes he did think my ideas were funny!) Two thousand emails later, the book is nearly done. And now I am, of course, thinking about the next project. If only I could sneak a peek at my Facebook page fifteen years in the future, maybe I'd get a better idea about what I should be writing!

Write Your Own *Tangled* Story: *Tangled* Creative Writing Prompts

1. Everything Book. Taking inspiration from Jena's everything book, keep your own journal of quotations that inspire you. Does collecting these sayings affect how you think about things? Is your everything book something you'd want to share with other people? Why or why not?

2. Loser with a Laptop. Write an entry for Owen's blog, Loser with a Laptop, using what you know about the characters in the story. You could describe something that happens in the first three sections of the novel from Owen's perspective, imagine something that happens before we meet the characters, or make up an event that happens after the book ends. Keep in mind that Owen loves his blog because, as he says, "I can be completely honest, can say the things that get stuck in my throat in my real life" (p. 228).

3. Imaginary Character. Jena and Dakota can't be the only ones who find Skye's notes about suicide. Imagine a story about someone else who finds a note Skye has written. How does that person react? What does he or she decide to do? Does your imagined character understand that Skye is trying to tell them "just how bad it can get" (p. 169)? Why or why not?

4. Imaginary Letter. Imagine the sorts of letters that Dakota and Shasta write each other. Compose a note from Dakota to Shasta. Through Dakota's voice, what can you show about the things that are important in his life? How is his relationship with Shasta helping him become more mature? How can this maturity reveal itself through his writing?

5. Tangled Angles. Skye begins to understand what happened to her father when she reads the email from Andres Oliveira; meanwhile, Skye's mother is oblivious to her daughter's realization (p. 199). Imagine another situation in which one person's entire world changes while the other person is doing something as banal as making watermelon soup. Take a page from Carolyn Mackler's multiperspective writing in *Tangled* and tell the story of what happens from both characters' perspectives.